MEET. CUTE.
AWKWARD.

for the queer at heart

ISBNs:
978-1-954214-35-4 (OpenDyslexic)
978-1-954214-36-1 (Déjà vu)
978-1-954214-37-8 (ePub)
978-1-954214-138-5 (Kindle)

Printed in the USA

CONTENTS

Trim

by Kayla Whittle

Val had inspected few shops as bright and chaotic as None and Sons Flower Emporium Extraordinaire, Welcome to All, Closed on Tuesdays. A tiny asterisk sat beside 'and Sons' on the crooked sign out front with a small addendum stating they no longer presumed only men could enter the family business and that actually one of the granddaughters ran the shop. That change hadn't been on the paperwork Val had picked up at her office, or else she might not have accepted this case. There were only two granddaughters who could have taken over the flower shop, and one had once been her best friend.

Her throat tightened, mouth dry. Val's nerves hadn't been this bad since her first round of inspections five years back, before she'd learned to like her job.

None and Sons Flower Emporium
Extraordinaire looked up to code on the
outside. Buckets overflowed with dazzling
blooms, lining the storefront with turquoise
and chartreuse and pink. The sidewalk
remained clear; no pixies nested in the
gutters. Those would have been minor
offenses, anyway; Val had unearthed worse
violations throughout her career. She'd fined
businesses hoarding endangered potions
ingredients and apothecaries that physically
trapped customers until they made a
purchase. Then there was her portal problem.
Unauthorized doorways connecting this semi-
mundane realm and its neighboring world.
Leaking magic couldn't be handled lightly.

Val fought the urge to comb through her
hair or turn back to where she'd parked her
car. She liked to make things orderly, and
safe, so her title as Magical Misconductor fit
well. She liked things familiar, so she stuck to
local assignments, afraid to try anything new
or travel too far. This was her last shop visit of
the day, and she'd never before passed a case
to someone else. This wouldn't be the first she
dropped, no matter how much nervous sweat
coated her palms. The sun hung low, warmth
curling around the back of her neck as Val
entered the shop.

The doors opened quietly, hinges well-oiled. Above hung a clearly marked exit sign. Ahead, it looked like a garden had overgrown and thrown itself onto the shop floor. Grass flattened beneath Val's sensible heels, the lawn spreading to coat every aisle. Vines clung to the walls, overgrown plants dangled in baskets hung from the ceiling, and snapdragons writhed near the register. Val stepped closer to inspect their cage, but something small and furred wrapped around her ankles.

She staggered backward, hands clenching into fists, but it was only a cat. White and fluffy, impossibly round. Her heart sank, prickled with sharp, icy dread.

"Hello, Martin," Val greeted him quietly, and in return he released a hideous shriek.

"Welcome!" The call came from somewhere behind the front counter. "Welcome to None and Sons and Also the Granddaughter. I'll be with you in a moment!"

Something crashed in the backroom; Val's hands tightened again. She eyed Martin and he opened his mouth wide, tongue lolling.

"We're having a sale on the peace lilies and the rage ones, too. Three for the price of— oh. You're unexpected."

Val knew this woman with leaves in her hair and dirt under her nails, eyes bright as tree bark and fresh soil. It'd been years but her voice remained the same, softened at the edges like a dessert left out too long in the heat. Years, and still her veins buzzed when their eyes met. Here was the classmate who'd helped Val find her voice before every school presentation and calmed her down afterward. Here was the friend who'd encouraged her to apply to college, to get that art degree, to try something new. They'd lost touch and grown apart, two blossoms separating so they wouldn't smother each other.

"Hi, Florian." Val gripped her clipboard, trying for a smile. The kind that said she'd thought about contacting Florian years ago when she'd moved back to town. The kind that admitted she'd been so scared of rejection she hadn't even tried.

"We prefer not to announce any inspections in advance," Val said. "It skews the results."

Val tugged at her collar when she noticed her old friend staring at the brassy double-M pinned there. She'd received it last year at the annual company party for Magical Misconductors and was embarrassingly proud of it.

"It's good to see you again," Florian said, offering her hand.

It was strange to look down on Florian, to have forgotten how short she was. To see her, ethereal and light and exactly the opposite of everything Val felt in her stiff work clothes. Val shook her hand to be polite, but didn't hold her grip for long; Florian's skin was warm, soft like a petal.

"Let me give you the tour," Florian said.

Together, they stepped down aisles filled with garden tools, spades and rakes and little houses for birds and gnomes and the least-troublesome variety of goblin. Past plants basking in a thick blanket of sunlight. Flowers bloomed and the taller plants preened within their pots. Val nudged a blossom with the end of her pen, pressing her lips together. Martin, Florian's cat, trailed behind them and hissed at the bloom when it growled.

"I know tiger lilies are territorial, but you need to trim these so no one will trip," Val said.

"Of course," Florian said, hovering over her shoulder. "Do you need to see the back, too?"

They went behind the counter; Val had expected to find at least one other employee in the backroom, but Florian was working alone.

"Most of the staff work in the greenhouses. They're off property, handling deliveries," Florian said. "I work the storefront."

Making a note of that, and sidestepping
Martin, Val peered inside the room. Too many
boxes were piled on the floor, crowding a bank
of sinks. Some of the corners were cobwebbed
with non-sentient species of spider. A door
opened to the backside of the building where a
dumpster rusted on crumbling asphalt. Val
tested the floorboards, digging her heels in
harder than necessary. She peered into bins
and found nothing amiss. Still, she caught the
sharp edge of Florian's relief when they
stepped back into the main room. It stung,
knowing their reunion made her old friend so
uncomfortable.

They paused by the register; the
snapdragons turned their blooms toward them
to eavesdrop.

"You'll receive a copy of my report in the
mail," Val said, the edge of her clipboard
digging into her side. "I don't see a need for
reinspection, but fix the issues you'll see
pointed out in the paperwork. Otherwise, the
next inspector might fine you."

"The next inspector?" Florian asked. "It
won't be you?"

"I suppose it might be," Val admitted. If
she didn't tell the office she knew Florian
None. "But there's no guarantee—"

Hesitantly, Val offered one of her business
cards to Florian. It stated Val's name and title

and phone number, no surname, no flourish, black ink printed on stark white. No one ever called her at the office; she knew the card would end up in the trash after she left.

"If you have any questions," Val explained when Florian glanced upward. "On the paperwork."

"Right. The paperwork," Florian said, dark eyes crinkling like they'd done years ago whenever something amused her. Val had always been able to make Florian laugh. It'd been one of her favorite things, how easily Florian took to happiness.

Val lowered her clipboard. "Florian—"

Over the florist's shoulder, through the doorway, the discarded boxes shifted. An outline appeared on the floor, lighting the shadowed space with a tinge of incandescent blue. The glow worsened as the illusion hiding the trapdoor faded, wood parting for a small, angry elf.

"Florian, you need to talk to Edgar, again. This is the third time this month my lunch *mysteriously* disappeared and you *know* I always label it—"

The rant fizzled out as the elf realized Florian had company. His gaze met Val's, then her Misconductor's badge, and then found the knife she'd pulled when the hidden door had opened. *This* was the true danger of her job, where she peered into the cracks of society and struggled to regulate them, alone. A portal, where there wasn't meant to be one. A tear between realms that could destabilize without proper care and maintenance.

The trapdoor swung closed with a heavy thump.

"Oh, Florian," Val disregarded her professionalism, disappointment strangling her tone. Because she *liked* Florian, and that offended her. "You have an unregulated portal?"

That meant closing down the shop immediately. It meant Val needed to retrieve her caution tape from her car's central console to coat the front entryway. It meant calling in a manager to investigate the severity of the breach and hoping Florian wouldn't put up a fight.

"Well," Florian said, then hesitated. "I really wish you'd finished up a minute earlier."

The next morning, a headache throbbed at Val's temples. She sat and stared at the cubicle walls pressing in around her. The clatter of keyboards melded with the hum of the water cooler and the occasional squeal of a file cabinet.

Her desk felt cluttered. To her right sat her clipboard, marked with her notes from the flower shop. To her left, a stack of unfinished reports.

Val liked her job, though she hadn't expected to. The mounds of paperwork were tedious, but the occasional threats to her life kept things interesting. She folded back page one of the report on a coffee shop she'd inspected before the florist's. The place was likely to burn down within the year unless significant safety protocols were enforced, considering the dragon they kept on staff. Val couldn't focus on the words, the empty black and white of her files, when her thoughts kept drifting back to colorful blooms. Nosy snapdragons.

Florian. Who'd cried once when Val gifted her a sketch she'd spent an absurd amount of time on. Who'd been the first to listen when Val stumbled over her realization that she didn't want to be close to anyone physically but still wanted romance so much it made her limbs ache.

Val's phone rang. Chairs squeaked and a mug clattered as her coworkers startled at the noise; Val cursed softly at her newly acquired papercut. Her phone rang again, shaking off a layer of dust before she answered it.

"You didn't report me yet," Florian said—
because of course it was Florian. That
windswept, breathy voice needed no
introduction.

"I haven't filed the paperwork yet," Val
said, which was a funny way to admit it.

"The store's closed," Florian said. "I've
been waiting for someone else to come poking
around it and, well, me."

Management was quick to look into
unregulated portals; often those who'd created
them used them to quietly slip away if they
were discovered. Val had heard it was quite
nice on the other side, where magic ran
unrestrained and things existed that couldn't
be understood or perceived by humanity. But
everyone knew stories about the unchecked
portals that went bad, the buildup that could
push and pull the opening's bounds and made
them likely to explode.

If Florian had fled, she wouldn't have been
able to call Val's office. Not even a sorcerer
could boost a phone connection that'd stretch
between realms.

"Is it possible you need to get a closer
look?" Florian asked. "For the paperwork."

Technically, it *would* improve Val's records
if she had more details. Portals were typically
a run-when-you-see-them affair, so inspectors
passed tips via word of mouth on how to best

spot them. Val cleared her throat, still aching
a little from all the shouting she'd done the
day before. Florian had stood there, nodding
along, while Val ranted about how serious
magical mismanagement was, and how she
was only a medium-ranking safety inspector
and how special exemptions couldn't be given
to None and Sons simply because they'd been
friends, once. Florian had listened. There'd
been no chasing or fighting or attempts to stab
Val in the back.

It'd made her shiver, because that was the
sort of thing she expected when she uncovered
something dangerous. It'd made her glare at
Florian through the shop door while she
covered it in caution tape.

It'd made her leave the clipboard on her
desk, untouched. Her headache persisted, but
warmth flared in her chest. After five years of
following regulations, this was something new.

"Yes," Val said. "I should make a closer
inspection."

They met first at the coffee shop two
blocks down from None and Sons, where Val
wasn't warmly welcomed after the lecture
she'd given their dragon. She held her first sip
in her mouth for a long moment, pulling the
coffee between her teeth to check for any

bitterness or unexpected residue. Other safety
inspectors had been poisoned for less.

Val pretended not to watch as Florian
ordered her tea, and added an awful amount
of sugar, and sighed deeply into her paper ·
cup.

"Look," Florian broke their silence when
they stepped out onto the sidewalk. "The
customers over there want flowers I grow
here, and the customers here want the flowers
I can only grow there. This is a logical
shortcut. I even keep a ledger on the other
side."

"Keeping your receipts means nothing,"
Val said, taking another drink of passively
aggressive lukewarm coffee. "All portals need
an approved regulator to document—"

"Do you know the going rate for a portal
regulator these days? Actually, you probably
do. You know it's more than a business this
size could afford," Florian said.

They paused outside None and Sons and
Val looked at the storefront, the crowded
windows filled with blooms and leaves and
growing things. Her caution tape, angry
stripes cutting across the door.

Regulators were expensive. It was
meticulous work, keeping a portal within its
boundary, and that was often reflected in the
price of maintenance fees. Val had considered

switching over to that department, tempted by the paycheck. The work was harder, and the other realm was wild and dangerous, but filled with the kind of magic that infiltrated songs and scripts and paintings.

"I'm not asking for any favors because you know me. Knew me. Not that you—you look good," Florian said, flushing, taking a long drink from her cup, hiding part of her face. "I only hoped you might see things from my family's perspective."

They entered the store around the back by the dumpster because there was less caution tape there. Several of the leaves caught in Florian's hair drooped as they neared the boxes covering the portal. Her posture had relaxed somewhat from the stiffness she'd held the previous day; maybe Florian's worry hadn't been over Val at all, but over her job title.

The look Florian shot her when they neared the false boxes was the same conspiratorial look they'd shared whenever they'd snuck out to feed stray pixies. It felt familiar in a way that unclenched something that'd been wound tight inside Val for a long time. It unsteadied her heartbeat when she needed to be sharp.

"Wow, that sure looks dangerous," Florian said when she realized Val had pulled out her blade again. "Is that necessary?"

"Is the connection between realms ripped into your stockroom floor necessary?" Val asked, feeling defensive.

"Yes," Florian admitted before she popped open the portal.

Val hesitated. If she entered after Florian, an ambush could wait on the other side. Entering first meant Florian could close the portal and leave her trapped in a place overrun with magic she didn't understand. The unknown loomed before her, stark and bright and terrifying. She thought about the last time she'd seen Florian, those nights before graduation where they'd been buzzing with anticipation and the promise to stay in touch. The moment, months later, when Val realized they'd both been lying. Not on purpose, but it meant losing someone she'd wrongly assumed she'd always have. It'd meant the end of something. It had been a long, long time since Val had looked at someone and thought that they felt like home.

It would be its own kind of thrill, to trust someone again. To feel less lonely.

"You first," Val said, prodding Florian through the trapdoor.

For a moment they were awash in blue, the glow striping their skin, catching the yellows and reds painted onto Florian's fingertips and the knife in Val's hand. Then they were on the other side, in another world, in another storeroom. Florian held out her hands, empty and unthreatening. They were alone.

Relief tugged at Val, because she didn't need to fight. Because with each passing moment, Florian felt more familiar, like the same girl Val had grown up alongside.

"This is probably one of the more boring cases you've investigated," Florian said, hefting an overstuffed binder from a nearby desk. There were more nearby, all neatly labeled to mark off quarterly earnings. Val pulled on a pair of gloves before she flipped one open, eyeing bills of sale and checked-off payment plans and scribbled inventory lists.

"Gloves?" Florian asked. She looked like she was trying hard to maintain a frown, but the edges of a smile kept breaking through. "Sorry, Val but my paperwork isn't poisonous."

"What?" Val's shoulders drew upward when she heard the choked-short sound of Florian's laughter. "I have every right to be cautious."

"I expected nothing less from the most careful person I know. The person who saved me from myself when I wanted to buy that secondhand potion in high school and you told me I should be more careful because I didn't know where those ingredients had been. Or stopped me when I nearly trampled over that pixie nest behind your house. Or asked me to reconsider when I wanted to ask out the witch down the street who had a habit of cursing her exes—"

"I get your point," Val said with a shake of her head, glancing over the rest of the room. It was neat, scrubbed clean, and through a nearby doorway Val saw the entrance to an enormous greenhouse. She moved closer, peering inside, eyes widening.

It was incandescent. Lovely. That was the only way to describe it. From where Val stood, the greenhouse appeared endless, with towering trees and greenery obscuring the walls while sunlight dazzled through the ceiling. Elves dug through flowerbeds, gently uprooting blooms that chimed softly when they were shifted. A spider, whispering to himself, wove a web between two ferns that released a soft pink fog whenever the webbing rattled them. In the distance, tree trunks moved stiffly, boughs dipped to sweep away stray cuttings and petals scattered across the floor.

There were no set aisles, no clear boundaries; it was all incredible, beautiful chaos. Like Florian. Remembering herself, Val looked back to the shopkeeper, who had a strange smile on her face. Like Florian had just caught sight of something she'd lost, but all she'd really been doing was staring at Val.

"Grandpa None really did well, didn't he?" Florian asked. "I've kept the family's facilities the same but like to think I've brought my own touch to the place."

Val didn't doubt it. That was an essential part of Florian, grasping things with potential and polishing them until they could hold their own shine. Turning, Val busied herself with shutting and locking the door to the greenhouse so she wouldn't need to look at Florian any longer.

"Have you spent much time on this side before?" Florian asked, seating herself at the desk. Sorting through paperwork, and shoving stacks in Val's direction every so often.

"No," Val said. "I don't take much vacation time."

"Probably for the best," Florian said. "My grandfather came here for a visit two years ago and then decided it was time for him to enjoy his retirement. But I didn't think I'd ever see you again after you left, either, so maybe there's hope for him, still."

Val thought of the messages she'd never sent and calls she'd never made. First because she'd been busy, and then guilty because time had passed by so quickly. Florian had been figuring out her own life, too, so maybe they both had their excuses, or maybe they both should have tried harder.

"Did you take over the shop when he left?" Val asked. "Do you like being a florist?"

"Yes," Florian smiled. "To both. I realized that just because this is the easy choice for me, that doesn't mean it isn't the one that'll make me happiest. This is mostly everything I've ever wanted."

There was a pause where Val thought she was meant to ask about the other things Florian dreamed of, to see which pieces of their childhood she could patch together with their shared memories of wishing. Val had been too angry and impulsive to stick to anything for long back then, though there'd been something satisfying about carving her mark down on paper; Florian hadn't committed to much either, but everything she did, she did fully. Hints of that stubborn strength clung to her vibrant storefront, nestled within each new growth sitting in the greenhouse.

"And you?" Florian asked. "Do you like being an inspector?"

"It's a good job," Val said. They both knew she hadn't gone to college with any intention of doing anything like this with her life. "It has its moments."

"Like now?" Florian nudged Val's side, laughing when she fumbled with her clipboard. "I missed you, Val. This town went a little grey when you left."

Val embraced the new warmth in her chest, when Florian urged her to sit in the chair beside hers. Their shoulders pushed together, pressure firm and steady and familiar, as they poured over the store's records.

Val went to None and Sons again the next day after she'd edited and uploaded and sent off the reports for the other shops she'd inspected. There was a stack of new assignments waiting for her, struggling for attention beside the lure of her pending case. Val couldn't stop thinking about it because of its importance, and how it put her career on the line, and every moment spent working on the case brought her closer to Florian.

"This *is* boring criminal activity," Val admitted, stretching her neck. Florian's hand ghosted over the back of it and Val tensed, but her grip was warm and soft and soothing. There was so much paperwork to look at, and usually Val didn't mind a challenge, but

Florian's grandfather had had his portal open for decades. The edges seemed secure, steady, but that was to Val's untrained eye.

"I know," Florian said with a sympathetic pat. "So many fae weddings where they want flowers that don't even glow or talk back to you."

There were pages of pixies who wanted baby's breath for their nests and humans wanting dragonroot for their feet and every kind of inconspicuous transaction of people buying illegal plants simply because they were pretty. Most magical plants were easiest to acquire on this side of the portal, thriving in the greenhouse. This realm had a certain shine impossible to replicate at home.

Martin stretched, paws kneading into Val's thigh as he rearranged himself on her lap.

"What's this?" Val asked, uncovering a list nailed to a bone-white clipboard. Each item was listed in red.

"Invasive species," Florian said. "I'm not going to be the one responsible for cross-contaminating worlds."

Responsible. That was the problem. Florian actually seemed responsible. Val had spoken to a few of the elves in the greenhouse and managed not to need her knife throughout her assessment, though one had tried bribing her to use it against the ogre stealing his lunch.

The workers seemed happy; Florian needed the extra income to get them their medical and miscellaneous magical benefits packages.

"Let's take a walk," Florian suggested, and Val agreed, too eager to stretch her legs.

They went into the greenhouse, past crackling fire lilies and a rainbow assortment of flowers, some with petals large enough for the elves on break to rest upon. Outside these walls, Val could only imagine what magic existed. In here, it created an impossible, alluring oasis. Sprites rearranged long-limbed plants topped with glowing orbs; vines writhed like eels across the irregular pathway, chasing each other and tumbling end over end.

"You've outdone yourself, Florian," Val said. "I've never seen a place like this before. You're—it's wonderful. I mean—I don't—"

"Wow," Florian said. "From what I remember, I wasn't often the one leaving you speechless. I'll take it as a compliment."

The greenhouse was beautiful, so Val hated it, because it made her work complicated. Policy stated she should have reported the incident days ago. It meant the storefront would close and Florian would never again be granted a business license on her home side of the portal. The family business would end, and every time Val passed the empty shop windows she'd have to think of Florian's leaf-strewn hair and Martin's incessant shedding and the fact that it'd all ended because of her.

"Have you made a decision yet?" Florian asked. "My delivery schedule is completely halted and the customers have started to call in with their concerns, due to the alarming amount of tape on the door and all."

"Soon," Val said, and hoped that now that she'd been given a second chance with Florian, she wasn't going to break that promise.

Soon meant scheduling meetings with management and fitting in appointments at other shops around discussions with Florian. Val's shin throbbed after a fight with a pair of sphinxes who'd been using riddle-filled vernacular to cover up a deficit in their taxes. She slumped at her desk, relying on that dragon-fired coffee, because deciding how she should follow the rules was thrilling and terrifying and sleep-depriving.

It had to end. Val wasn't known for procrastinating even on difficult cases. Florian None seemed happy in her store, and her portal was helping people on both sides. It'd been open for decades and hadn't collapsed yet; the Nones had to be doing something right. Val's decision could crush her friend—

not the girl she'd known in the past, but the woman she knew *now*. There was only one choice she could make.

Her phone rang, and someone in the cubicle next to her sputtered out a choked cough. Val's jaw tightened until her teeth ached.

"So?" Florian asked when Val answered her call. "You've been gone most of the week. It feels off, not having you around here."

"It's over, I think," Val said. "I should be able to meet you tonight. We have a few things we need to discuss."

"Dinner?" Florian suggested.

"I'll choose the place," Val said.

When she hung up, her stomach fluttered, not unlike the way it did whenever her life was threatened.

The None and Sons file had thickened with printouts and assessments, notations and recommendations. She set aside a sketch she'd made of Florian's greenhouse on the other side—at least, how it had appeared in one moment, because it would have shifted and grown by the next. Val neatly stacked the rest of the paperwork together and took it with her into her manager's office.

They went to a small place across town where Val and Florian had sometimes spent their lunchbreaks during high school, sharing plates of fries and ignoring the glare of the gorgon behind the counter. When Val stepped inside, she saw how the red booths had started to peel, and how a human leaned behind the register now, and how Florian stretched her arms wide to get Val's attention.

"The thing is, I can't take the suspense anymore," Florian said. "Soon it won't matter if you shut us down officially. I'm losing enough now that it'd take the rest of the quarter to recover, even if I reopened tomorrow."

She gulped down a mouthful of her milkshake, sliding over an identical one. Nudging the plate of fries, too, that sat between them. Val ignored both, too unsettled to eat.

"I apologize for the delay," Val said.

"Don't use your customer service voice," Florian scoffed. "Not with me. I'm grateful I'm not already shut down permanently. Or fined. Gods, you people love your fines."

"Money is usually the easiest way to get people to pay attention," Val frowned, pinching one of the fries. "Money was the issue to begin with, wasn't it?"

Portal regulators were pricy because they promised quality and safety in a way that protected more than one world.

Florian leaned closer, chewing on her straw.

"Something's different about you," she realized. "Where's your pin?"

Shifting uncomfortably—which happened often, in her stiff business casual—Val rubbed at her collar. There was a little hole left behind where she usually pinned her brass award, her recognition as a Magical Misconductor.

"They fired you?" Florian guessed. "I'll write to the office, tell them it was my fault—"

"No, Florian," Val interrupted. "They don't know how long I dawdled over the details of None and Sons, so please don't inform them of *my* misconduct."

She slid her clipboard over to Florian so she could have a look, and then tried to look busy pretending her heart wasn't racing. How many years had passed since she'd done something bold, something new? Val felt the sting of her nerves, drawing so tight they nearly covered her excitement. It became impossible to smother her smile when she saw the way Florian's expression cleared, eyes brightening.

"Regulator training?" Florian read off the pamphlet clipped to the front of Val's notes. "Val, you didn't."

"Switch departments?" Val asked. "Tell them I knew the perfect location where I could start? Of course I did. It's the next logical step in my career, anyway, and while you won't necessarily be getting the *best* service I can guarantee my rates will be—"

"Perfect," Florian smiled. "Absolutely perfect."

Val couldn't help but flush at the way Florian looked at her. It had been work, getting the department to think the None and Sons portal had merely been overlooked, through no fault of the florists. To management, the flower shop was finally getting the service they'd been waiting on for an indeterminate amount of time.

Val sputtered when Florian grabbed her by the lapel, pulling her close enough to knock over one of the milkshakes. It would stain, and she was flustered by all the hugging Florian was doing, but Val realized she didn't care. Not in that moment when things felt right and the future felt open. Like maybe they couldn't have the same friendship they'd once had, but there could still be something good between them. Val didn't necessarily want *friendship* anyway, and from the way Florian took Val's hand afterward, she thought the florist felt the same. Her grip was warm and strong and sure, like something beautiful that'd just taken root.

The Oak I Knew

Jacob Budenz

"Why do the birds go on singing?
Why do the stars glow above?
Don't they know it's the end of the world?
It ended when I lost your love."—The
Carpenters

You could say a hurricane took him from me,
although that wouldn't quite be right. Oak:
shaggy and slender and short, my pint-sized
Jesus, as I liked to call him. I didn't exactly
lose him to the hurricane alone. Not that he
was mine to lose. This is not a love story. At
least, not the kind you think.

    Morning, the day before the storm, I sat
across the fire from Oak at the edge of the
forest behind our house, while he bent over
the flames to make breakfast for our half of
The Compound. The sky? That ominous clear
that could only precede one thing. Even the

greenish morning haze, one of the ghosts of our ancestors' excess, had burned away early in the swell of the November sun. The weather was fine, if muggy, but we knew that the next night, we'd be huddled in our houses, felled trees clanging against The Shell, the metal half-dome we erected for every major storm. Uncle M had never been wrong about the weather.

I attempted to entertain Oak: "You know, they used to name each hurricane that hit the shore, and even some that never made landfall." With too few humans left on earth to form any real sense of collective history, it was my role at The Compound to research what society had been like before The Great Thaw, so we could learn from their discoveries and mistakes.

"Like human names?" Oak said, a dubious smile spreading his short-cropped beard to the boundaries of his thin face. He cracked an egg as big as his head into the cast iron pan, which sat on a grate above licking flames. Ostriches were one of the few birds bearing edible eggs that survived The Great Thaw, thanks to these facilities called "zoos" which displayed living animals for our ancestors' entertainment. Each ostrich egg fed ten. After my careful research about ostrich care, we'd determined they were worth breeding since we had a hundred adults at The Compound and about half as many children.

"Yeah, human names."

"If we started naming hurricanes, we'd run out by the end of the y—"

A screen door slammed nearby. We both glanced at the nearest house to see Uncle M striding toward us. Uncle M: sexagenarian, lover of our ancestors' gadgets, secret-but-not-so-secret holder of the belief that society's acceptance of queers like me had led to The Great Thaw, the scores of hurricanes each year, the tornadoes tearing across continents bearing flaming trash and molten plastic, the hilly coasts turned to clusters of tiny islands. Of all the things to have survived The Great Thaw, the occasional belief in this particular version of a god had never made sense to me. They'd gotten their Armageddon, but it hadn't turned out remotely the way they'd said it would. Wasn't that proof enough? But no, one of the first books I'd had to salvage had been a Bible—quite a feat to find such a work with all those tiny letters unmarred with water damage—and a handful of those who had lived before the great flood gathered every seven days to look at it, had even begun to indoctrinate some of the children. I guess everyone needed *something* to cling to.

Oak flipped the enormous egg, then waved cheerfully at Uncle M with a faded, pinkish-red oven mitt. My closest friend had a way of diffusing moods with that wide, friendly smile of his.

I half-raised my hand in greeting. Uncle M didn't deserve the energy required for a full wave. We were all about conservation at The Compound.

"Storm's coming. How you boys faring," he said, flatly, not seeking a reply.

"Oh, you know," said Oak. Flashing me a sidelong smile, he launched into a painstakingly detailed account of the day so far, from the friskiness of the ostriches in their pen at dawn to his ideas about the naming of hurricanes. Our private game: how far could Oak, beloved workhorse of The Compound, stretch Uncle M's patience? He'd just begun to explain his thoughts on the morning haze when Uncle M finally cut him off.

"I have a favor to ask of you," he said. "Confidential."

"Of me?" I said, winking at Oak. We all knew he wouldn't act this polite if he needed something from *me.*

I saw Uncle M's eyebrows, orange with traces of white hair, pinch as he considered some emasculating reply. But he wasn't stupid enough to insult me in front of Oak if he needed a favor.

"Actually," he said, hands folded over his crotch in false meekness. "This is a job for Oak. It might be a bit too…" he grasped for words, but it was too late.

"Manly for me? Too technical? Too… heterosexual?"

"I wasn't going to say that."

"Don't worry," I said, voice dripping with honey. "You can mutter it to me later, when Oak's not around. I'll leave you two alone."

I blew a kiss at Uncle M and stalked across the grass, making eye contact with Oak and pantomiming masturbation with three flicks of the wrist. This broke my friend's neutral mask just enough for a single snort of laughter.

If anyone should find what I've made of my journals and accuse me of oversensitivity, know that Uncle M had been, at the time, launching quiet warfare on the utility of my work. Never mind that I always got my share of chores done before I set out. Never mind that he owed so many of his gadget-tinkering skills to engineering books I'd acquired. Never mind that The Compound wouldn't know half of what we knew about weather, nutrition, agriculture, even the politics of collective living without my research. Never mind the incredible peril I risked in traveling to The

Archipelago, the hilly coastal metropolis
turned into a string of little islands rife with
toxic waste and turf wars among The Great
Thaw's survivors. Never mind the physical
demands of these trips to often-flooded
libraries: diving through pools full of plastic
that might wrap around your legs and drag
you into the depths, climbing over the rubble
of fallen buildings like a mountaineer.

No, to Uncle M, books were for the idle.
He'd drop hints of this to our cohabitants here
and there, manipulate the chore charts to
make it more difficult for me to get out to The
Archipelago unless he needed a particular
engineering book or some religious text, in the
name of "pulling my weight."

From the corner of my eye, I saw Uncle M
move toward him, his gut bulging behind his
light blue shirt, gesturing with rehearsed
precision. Oak, a head shorter than him and
bone-thin, stared at Uncle M without moving,
save for running his fingers through his long
mane of brown hair, like he did whenever he
was biting his tongue. And he bit his tongue
often enough.

That evening, when it came time to erect
The Shell, I positioned myself near Oak to coax

the contents of the whole "confidential" conversation out.

The Shell, a dome of aluminum and steel, consisted of six massive curved trapezoids which we attached to foundations that surrounded the outskirts of The Compound, the short ends of the trapezoids pointing outward like a lotus flower (another living beauty now found only in moldy picture books). By a system of pulleys, we pulled the short ends to the top of six beams in the center of The Compound, on top of which we fastened the seventh piece to cover the hole on top. Several people on ladders stood at the top of the beams to fasten all the pieces in place. The Shell was lined with tiny holes so we could breathe, and the Compound sat atop a hill where flooding was not a concern. I'd discovered its blueprints, invented by our ancestors too late to make a difference, and a team of us at The Compound salvaged the materials we needed from the suburbs of The Archipelago to create it. It was quick to erect and nearly impenetrable. Though not perfect by any means, The Compound was safe. Safer than any life I could envision since The Great Thaw.

I stood next to Oak as we hoisted up one of the curved trapezoids.

"So, M has this machine that harnesses lightning and stores it as electrical power," Oak said. It took very little coaxing. "It's a sort of lightweight tower."

"Okay," I said. Electrical power. A fickle thing with an unquenchable thirst for resources—one of the main excesses that helped bring about The Great Thaw. So, of course, Uncle M had what they used to call a *hard-on* for it. "And?"

Oak kept pulling his rope without looking at me. "He wants me to try it out."

"So you'll set it up and call it a day?" But I knew something was wrong. He couldn't keep a secret from me, after all the time we'd spent together.

"What's the problem? What are you not telling me?" While we waited for the next command to pull, I let my thumb rest against his knuckle in assurance. Before you jump to conclusions, no. We were simply comfortable with each other. Sure, I'd done an awful lot to convince myself he wasn't my "type," all twig-thin and lean muscle, but mostly Oak didn't swing that way, as far as I knew. I'd never detected any interest from him, toward me or any other man in The Compound.

We heaved. The tip of our trapezoid reached the top of the two beams, and we held fast while men on ladders latched our part of

The Shell into place. Above, plump clouds tinted with purple and orange sailed by at an alarming pace, as if to outrun the coming storm.

Oak sighed. "The tower has to be set up offshore. Something about how lightning hits the water and spreads, and how it's more likely to strike the tower with nothing else around."

"What? But you'd have to leave—"

"Before dawn, if I'm going to make it to any kind of shelter. I'm supposed to wait out the storm in The Archipelago. Apparently the tower collapses, and it's light enough for me to drag down the hill by myself. Some sophisticated thing from before The Great Thaw."

Above, a metallic clang told us our portion of The Shell was secure. My hands burned when I released the rope. For a moment, my fingers wouldn't unfurl, as if I'd been holding so tightly, for so long, that I'd forgotten how to let go.

"You're not going, are you? I mean, he can't make you do something like that without a vote."

"Well, said he'd hold an emergency vote tonight, if I didn't agree. There's no point. The elders are on his side." The elders—our snarky name for Uncle M's generation, who held a silent majority when it came to major decision-making at The Compound.

From the sound of Oak's voice, I guessed he hadn't put up much of a fight, as was his way. Well, that was why he had me.

I spied Uncle M through the space between two houses, by the animal pens at the edge of The Shell, his hands on his hips, apparently "supervising." I marched toward him, ignoring Oak's cry of "Wait!" behind me. I knew he wouldn't follow.

"What the fuck is this all about?" I said in mock friendliness when I was close enough.

Uncle M swung around toward me, all feigned obliviousness, as if I hadn't caught him glance twice at me approaching and look performatively away before I could meet his eye. "Oh, we're just bringing the oxen—"

"Not that. Walk with me."

"I'm a little busy," he said, flicking his eyes nervously around for some excuse. "Shouldn't you be—?"

"Shouldn't you?" I snapped.

We walked. That was the thing about underhanded people like him: when pressed directly, they caved.

"What you're asking Oak to do is suicide." I was good at pressing. Not so much at subtlety.

"Don't be dramatic," he said. "I'm sure you can survive the night without him."

I ignored the jibe. "Why him? Why not one of *you?* Anyone else? Me?" That last word hung for a moment, a silent dare. I hadn't quite formed the thought, but something told me this was about something beyond electrical power.

"He's the only one with the strength and technical know-how—"

"I've read all the same books—"

He talked over me. "—to pull it off. Nobody from my generation would last out—"

"Let me go instead."

This actually managed to stop him, both from talking and from walking.

I continued, "Any mechanical stuff you and Oak know came from books I found."

"It's more than just curling up by the fire with a book in your hand. You—"

"I've been to The Archipelago more than anyone here. If anyone knew where to find shelter—"

"Then you can give Oak some pointers. Look, it's too late. I'd have to clear it with everyone in The Compound—"

"Like you did with Oak? Or are you pretending he volunteered?"

"Don't be stupid, Carl," he finally growled. And there it was. You play dumb long enough with cowards like Uncle M, it's amazing how direct they suddenly become. "One of you had

to go, and unfortunately, we don't have
another archivist. There are those here who
value what you do too much, Lord knows
why."

"Wait, what?" This time, I wasn't playing
dumb.

"Believe me, I wish it could be you. At least
Oak tries to hide *whatever it is* going on
between you two, and he's a hard worker. But
a few of the others said we have plenty of
hands," he sighed, and then said pointedly,
"and *we* can always make more hands." By
"the others," of course, I assumed Uncle M
meant those of his generation, the silent
majority, but I couldn't be sure of anything at
this point.

"I don't understand," I said, which was to
say I didn't want to understand. "We're not
even..." And anyway, so what if we were?
There was no law against it at The Compound,
last I'd checked. The first law of The
Compound was to value survival above all else
which meant, tacitly, valuing human life in
every form. All my life I'd believed this. All my
life I'd believed it kept me safe, kept us all
safe, to value each other in this way.

As if he heard my thoughts, he said simply,
"The survival of our species depends on its
ability to reproduce."

I stared at him, awestruck.

He continued, in his normal, mockingly reasonable voice: "Now, there are *children* in The Compound who look up to you both, for whatever reason..."

I heard nothing else he said. I saw torches in my periphery as others lit the evening work. I heard distant laughter and the pounding of my own blood. And I surprised both of us by punching Uncle M in the face.

I'll admit, I had no idea what I was doing. I'd been aiming for his nose, but I must have nicked just next to his eye, because only half my fist throbbed with pain. As he reeled back, caught off-guard, I wondered, *Am I supposed to hit him again?* But punching had hurt more than I'd expected, so I settled for a kick to his crotch, except I missed and kicked his hip instead. Still, he went toppling over with a satisfying grunt.

Others were quickly upon me, those people with torches, dragging me away before I could get another word in.

We didn't have prison at The Compound. In the rare occasion of major wrongdoing, you were taken back to your home where your housemates had to keep watch outside the house for three days. Beyond your own forced isolation, four other people slept outside during that time, suffering worse than you did, angry as hell by the end of it. It was extremely efficient punishment, shame. In the past, our ancestors held one another captive for years, sometimes lifetimes. They even killed their own for certain transgressions. The idea of murder had been drilled into our heads as unfathomable, here at The Compound where survival was god and loss was luxury. And I had believed it—all my life I had believed that The Compound valued life above all else. Yet here went our elders, sneakily sending Oak to die, to set an example that *certain* behaviors would not be tolerated. Evidently, the possibility of romance between two men was more of a threat to the survival of The Compound than some cloak-and-dagger execution by way of a mission doomed to fail, more of a threat to survival than the precedent such an execution entailed. How could anyone begin to make that distinction? To say that the net good a person could do for their community would be nullified by the harm they'd caused—or in this case, *the harm their example would cause?* Was it so likely that all the children in our community would see two grown men together and decide to forego reproduction when they themselves grew up? I didn't think so; before I had the refuge of books to teach me there was nothing unnatural about what I desired, I'd developed my attraction with nothing but examples to the contrary. And Oak? Well, now, I wondered if I'd ever be able to ask him.

Thus, I spent the following days alone, holed up in a house large enough for six roommates, like the lonely ghost wandering the halls of the haunted mansion in those gothic novels I snuck back from The Archipelago for Oak sometimes. Except the houses in The Compound were a single story, so there were no grand spiral staircases for me to sail up and down, no great halls through which my otherworldly moans could echo. The worst part was that I couldn't give Oak "some pointers," as Uncle M had put it. I couldn't even draw out a map, clue him in on spots in the Archipelago with the most shelter. I was cut off. I couldn't even say goodbye to him before he went out on an errand that might end his life, let alone hedge his bets for survival. Leaving the safety of The Shell during a hurricane. It was criminal!

The first night, I yearned for him in a way I didn't know I could yearn. I obsessed over the thought that if only *Oak* had socked Uncle M in the face, something he would never do, they'd have had no choice but to confine him for the hurricane. Then, if Oak survived, which it seemed like nobody expected, what would be next? Would we have to move into separate houses? Avoid each other? Because we were *a threat to survival?* My mind turned and turned all night, over the knowledge that my friend was essentially being punished because of my sexuality. That sexuality had become punishable at all.

The next morning, I awoke to a loud clang and perfect blackness. The Shell had been sealed. I imagined Oak out at sea by now, staring out over the filthy water toward coming storm clouds, wind whipping around him.

I bumped around the house, feeling along the walls and knocking crotch-first into furniture, until I found last night's dinner ration left for me just inside the front door: cold porridge accompanied by a reasonably fresh hunk of bread. I'd like to say that the food turned to ash in my mouth from missing Oak, that with Oak gone, maybe never to return, I couldn't scare up an appetite. But I ate it on the spot, right there, on my knees. I was starving, and it was good even cold.

Out there, I could hear the crackling of morning fires, the outbursts of laughter, the voices of my cohabitants. Who else was behind this? Who else had betrayed Oak so thoroughly?

And another, admittedly selfish question had begun to nag me: Who else had seen something I hadn't in Oak's behavior toward me? And were they right? Was there something between us?

I got up, stumbled through the dark to Oak's room, and found his guitar, a ratty thing I'd found for him at The Archipelago. I sat there on the floor of his bedroom, twanging out shaky chords, surrounded by the smell of him. I could hardly manage the basics he'd taught me, less so in the dark. But when all you've got to do is think, thinking is last thing you want to do. I imagined he was there with me, patiently correcting the placement of my fingers with his own, as he'd done so often before, a gesture so simple and sincere that I'd never thought anything of it. But it was too hard. I was just no good at the guitar. I never had been.

I began to cry, softly, at first with the frustration of trying to force music out of the unyielding instrument. In the thick shadows of the empty house, a lifelong friendship of tiny intimacies, maddening in their ambiguity, unfolded before me. One of my earliest memories: child-Oak reaching a slender hand out to help me, and only me, across a filmy stream of red-tinted water in the forest before we ran to catch up with the other orphan

children of The Compound. Sunsets after a
long day of tilling as teenagers, after I'd grown
far taller and bigger-boned than he, I would
carry him on my back from the modest fields
at the edges of The Compound, his sharp
cheekbone pressed against the back of my
neck and the warm, slow breath of his half
sleep itching at my sunburned shoulders. And
so on. As with Oak's unsuccessful attempts to
teach me music, I'd ignored the light tug in my
abdomen every time, never daring to name it
even before I knew it had a name.

    I set his guitar aside. I ate. I napped. I
longed. And yes, I wept more than I'd care to
admit. I stopped trying to keep track of time
until I heard the first crack of thunder and
figured it must be evening. The first arms of
the storm were swinging by us.

    I slept in Oak's bed, enveloping myself in
his blankets and the comforting smell of his
dried sweat. At times I half-dreamed he lay
there with me; at times, awake, I pictured him
setting up inane machines in the tormented
sea, and in those moments I tried to force
myself back beneath the tide of dreaming. If
Uncle M had been right about him, if there
had been something between us I'd simply not
allowed myself to see... It was too much to
bear.

Does dwelling on that last possibility—that I might be losing the only shot at love and intimacy I might ever have *on top of* losing my best friend, *on top of* losing any faith I had in the community that was supposedly keeping me says—while my friend might still have been out there, while I might still have a shot at helping him, seem a little selfish to you? Well, then you're not the only one. Even as I pitied myself I chided myself for not thinking happier thoughts about my gentle friend, as if the least I could do while trapped in here was picture calm shores for Oak, imagine his safety, his long fingers gripping his canoe as he dragged it uphill in triumph. But each time I pictured those long fingers I couldn't help but see them entwined in mine, and the cycle would repeat.

The final day and a half of my confinement was the worst. When The Shell came down, afternoon sunlight streaming through the windows, I still had no way of knowing whether Oak was all right. The Compound strictly prohibited communication with anyone in confinement except in emergencies. Although I wanted to believe Oak would find some way to tell me he'd made it home safe, I knew it would've been unwise of to risk any more on our behalf. So came the maddening pendulum: hope that he'd survived, certainty that he hadn't. He was Schrödinger's cat: both

alive and not, both in love with me and not.
Only I was the one in the box. Believe me—I
burned for him by then. I'd really talked
myself into being in love with Oak, now that he
was gone.

I did know, since nobody came to fetch me,
that the hurricane had done no meaningful
damage to our community—or at least to our
property. Our ancestors had designed The
Shell's technology well, even though they'd
discovered their need for such protection far
too late to make any real difference in the fate
they'd set in motion.

That morning, I felt more charity toward
their timing than ever before.

When I was allowed to leave on the
evening of my third day, none of my
housemates guarded the front door, not even
standing there with their arms crossed to guilt
me for their having to stand outside day and
night. Everyone sat in a circle at the center of
The Compound. A Circle, where everyone in
The Compound old enough to make a decision
gathered. I scanned the Circle for Oak, not
finding him. I joined the Circle myself,
squeezing in between two women. I fought
tears. He wasn't here. He hadn't returned.

None other than Uncle M walked around the inside of the ring of rapt faces, waffling: "...definitely unfortunate, but he insisted on being the one to go. We haven't heard from him since he left us before the storm. So we can only assume he didn't make it."

There was only one person he could've been talking about. My face burned. It was a sham! It was a sham, and everyone played along, nodded gravely like they actually believed him. The elders wouldn't be so bold as to come out and say, "We made an example of him." But they had. Uncle M told me they had, and in the shadows, regardless of what he was saying out in the open, this wriggling bottom feeder, "Uncle" to us all, would make it known what had really happened and why.

I watched the proceedings of the Circle numbly, watched the illusion of *collectivism* for what it was: a play performed by its own writers, its own directors, who could barely be bothered to deliver their lines with any real conviction. Except nobody, not even the elders who had set it in motion, seemed to see it as such.

"But here's the thing, friends," Uncle M continued in his brief and insincere eulogy. Friends! Without a trace of irony. "The tower could still be out there. The weather's fair, friends. And if my calculations are right—and

they haven't failed us yet, have they,
friends?—if my calculations are right, let's not
let the last act of this treasured member of our
community be in vain! With the amount of
electricity that device should have harnessed,
there's no telling what we could build! How
much progress we could make!"

"Here, here!" someone actually shouted.
Others followed, and not just the elders. My
god, he was really getting away with this.
Were they really going to trample over the
body of our hardest worker, our sacrificial
lamb, to take advantage of the stupid machine
he'd been manipulated into dying for? I'd
never seen Uncle M so eloquent before, so
capable of seizing a moment and saying all the
right things, out in the open in front of
everyone. He must have had help. He hadn't
written this script alone.

"It won't take much," he said, arms spread.
"Just one or two—"

"I'll go," I shouted, rising amidst the
scandalized murmurs of the crowd. The
homosexual had emerged from his chrysalis to
stir things up again.

Uncle M opened his mouth as if to protest,
but I continued, "Who else knows the coast as
well as I do? And The Archipelago? If Oak's
still out there, lost or unconscious or worse..."
I paused for effect, sweeping my gaze over the

circle, dodging Uncle M's eyes. "Who'd know better where to look?"

I'd like to say there was thunderous applause, but even if anyone had clapped, it would have been a hundred people in the open air on a windy day. Triumph looked more like many thoughtful glances, then a vote by a show of hands in which even most of the elders consented. "Makes sense," someone said, and I wasn't sure whether this person was hoping I, too, would fail, or if they recognized that although were weren't talking about it, Oak had been sent on his fool's errand because of his friendship with me. Either way, I was grateful. Others nodded along. I was to leave at dawn.

Afterward, hardly anyone spoke to me, especially not the men. I didn't blame them after what happened to Oak because of me. I took my dinner by one of the fires, sitting alone on damp grass, watching people I'd known my whole life talk around me as if I were a ghost. If there's no one to notice we're here, what are we if not ghosts? I'd spent my life believing the people around me were all that could keep me safe, doing everything I could to keep them safe, too. To value our survival above all else. It didn't feel like "ours" anymore. I went to bed early.

Sunrise. I made my way downhill in the hazy green of the morning pollution, walking down toward the coast without fanfare or farewell. I took little with me, dragging a canoe full of enough food for a couple days, Uncle M's drawing of the lightweight disk attached to its retractable tower, and of course, my notebooks. I of all people understood the importance of cataloguing experiences; as an archivist, I hoped at least in some small way I could contribute to the understanding of future generations, not just through the books I took notes on, but by journaling furiously, when I could find a free moment, about the things that happened to me. There are reasons to keep writing, even when the world has fallen apart. There was no telling who would stumble across something, be helped by it, like how the farmers who kept record of their goings-on never could have known they'd help keep the human race alive long after their own demise.

Anyway, I like to write. I think I'm pretty good at it.

It didn't take a genius to get to the coast from The Compound. The line of trees to my left ensured that I was going in a straight line. I thought pityingly of Oak, dragging a supposedly "light" metal contraption along with his canoe, a death march with two crosses to bear, one metal, one plastic. Dragging the canoe was awkward enough, and after the hurricane, an abundance of errant branches and tree trunks stood in my way. Even the mild November sun pounded into my back an hour in, the kind of sun we did our best to shield ourselves from, that pounded down even more fiercely, cancerously, than it had in our ancestors' day. And other dangers lurked in this peaceful, post-storm landscape. Errant gale-force winds could whip around me at any moment, flinging the worst of the debris at my unprotected head. Though we seldom worried about dangerous wildlife—so little remained that there was little statistical possibility of running into any large beasts— the kinds of creatures that survive an apocalypse as thorough as The Great Thaw are accustomed to extreme conditions to begin with: scorpions and gila monsters who suddenly find their desert domains spreading might spill over into even the grassiest of hills. All these and more we risked when we left The Compound, and frequent visits to The Archipelago hadn't made me utterly blithe to them. Oak, surely, even less.

Still, a different existential threat occupied my mind as I scanned the debris for anything that crawled, bit, stung. Supposing Uncle M's battery contraption was still intact, did I destroy it for revenge? Or did I bring it home safely, winning back the favor of the folks at The Compound? Did I return to the only safe place I'd ever known? Pull back the curtain, shine a light on the strings wrapped around the wrinkled fingers of our elders (I think that's how puppets work—I've only ever read about them)? I had to hope that others would listen, that enough of us with open eyes could set things right, to value the human life in front of us before its propagation.

And then there was the absurd hope that Oak was still alive, lost somewhere in The Archipelago. What then? We couldn't exactly walk back arm in arm and hope we'd seen the end of it. And no, I wasn't in denial. I'd accepted that he was dead the moment he'd said he was leaving. I might have been in love with a dead man. Still, I had hope.

I made it to the coast by the afternoon. Putrid water lapped the grass. The line of trees at my left continued into the sea, each tree further beneath the waves until their shaggy tops poked through the oily surface of the ocean, through the plastic and paper and filth our ancestors left us with. I'd read of beaches, even seen photographs of them: strips of land at the edge of the water covered

in rocks and shells that the rolling waves had
pulverized into a fine grain. Our ancestors
used to lie semi-nude at the water's edge
getting skin cancer so the sun would change
the shade of their skin. Surveying the grassy
slope interrupted by stinking grayish water,
where bottles bobbed atop the sea foam—the
beaches of old were all underwater, by then—I
smiled at the thought that anyone would spend
their time around this enormous toxic trash
receptacle.

The biggest danger of rowing to The
Archipelago was hardly what you'd expect of a
massive climate apocalypse; as far as we
knew, no hideously mutated, violent beasts of
leviathan-like proportions had risen from the
ashes of civilization, waiting to drag its
stragglers to the depths. Capsizing, however,
is a very real concern, and it's the reason
sending Oak out during a hurricane was so
obviously a death sentence. Capsizing most
likely meant that you and your paddle would
be tangled in one of the endless webs of
plastic waste, unable to grab hold of your
vessel in time to right it as the current
snatched it away. And these creatures our
ancestors had named jellyfish—which were
neither fish nor made of any kind of gelatin—
were one of a handful of living beings we knew
about that had truly thrived in the warming of

the seas. These graceful, delicate creatures sometimes drifted through the webs of plastic in equally flimsy swarms, and a critical mass of them merely brushing up against you, depending on its species, could range in results from excruciating pain to paralysis to cardiac arrest. No matter how many times I'd rowed this path, my blood still spiked each time a larger wave rolled beneath me.

Uncle M had instructed Oak to row the battery tower out about two miles offshore, halfway between the edge of the trees and The Archipelago. Once I got my canoe over the mounds of junk metal, tangled plastic bags bearing words like "HappyMart" and "THANK YOU!"—*Thank you for bringing civilization closer to its inevitable destruction!*—it was a straight shot. The farther out I went, the less trash floated about, but it was always with me, like a shadow. Plastic waste: the ghost of our ancestors that wouldn't go away—except unlike the ghosts in the old storybooks, the plastic wouldn't go away no matter how much we atoned for our ancestors' earthly blunders.

Except the tower wasn't there. I paddled about halfway to the Archipelago. No net-like tower of lightweight metal, expanded like an accordion, swayed in the waves. Behind me: the rolling hills of the coast rose on the horizon. Ahead of me: The Archipelago's spires pierced the air. Around me: nothing but the trash. I hadn't really prepared for the possibility of turning up completely empty-handed. A number of things could've happened. Uncle M could've undershot the length of the anchor's chain. The storm's winds could've been too strong for it. Or, of course, the storm could've beat Oak to the coast. Would he have gone for it anyway, resigning himself to his fate, capsizing in the white-capped waves while he towed the collapsed tower on its floating disk behind him? I wasn't ready to consider that just yet.

I paddled toward The Archipelago, where I'd start by looking for the tower on the shorelines—and maybe, by way of finding that, Oak. The tower would be a start. I couldn't exactly ask around, *Hey, have you seen this man whose features bear striking resemblance to whitewashed images of the Christ?* Not that many around here would've seen a painting of our ancestors' "savior" or known what they were looking at if they had. They'd think me some sort of post-apocalypse preacher, and anyway, they'd probably frisk me for supplies. How to describe the people of The Archipelago? They were, well... conditions were tougher out there. I'd once had to surrender the books I'd found to a woman bearing a machete, who demanded them for

kindling. Kindling! Can you imagine? I knew
better than others at The Compound, who
painted this picture of the dwellers of this
decayed city as savages, as cannibals, even.
But really, they were brutal pragmatists. I'd
seek shelter and search for the tower and, hey,
even Oak, in the morning.

What used to be a city of tall hills now rose
from the trash-riddled sea, like the mottled
spine of a great beast who'd drowned beneath
the waves or perhaps slept, waiting to rise.
The central islands provided the highest
ground and, therefore, the best shelter. I
navigated through narrow channels flanked on
either side by broken-down houses on hills,
built so close together they looked squished.
Little flitting shapes wove through the beams
of porches and in the shadows behind broken
windows: cats, the only creatures native to the
city to survive The Great Thaw, who no doubt
licked the bones of every human corpse clean
years ago. One of the little islands featured
homes burned utterly to their foundations,
with a single house inexplicably standing.

Back then, cities were like fortresses to
protect against the untamable wilderness.
Now, compared to the placid planes that
surrounded The Compound, The Archipelago
was the real wilderness.

I searched with little plan. The problem was that Oak didn't know The Archipelago like I did. I could search the most logical hideouts, the buildings with the strongest foundations or the little buildings sheltered from the wind in the shadow of larger ones, but Oak wouldn't know what to look for, especially if he'd come here in the desperation of escaping an ever-intensifying hurricane. I spent most of the day searching the concrete shores for a washed-up canoe. Also, for a body. I found neither.

By dusk, in need of a morale boost and a place to sleep, I reached one of my favorite little islands. High on a hill, through overgrown woods, was a space called a "botanical garden," where our ancestors planted all sorts of crazy exotic vegetation and built pathways so they could wander around, feeling connected to the natural world that they slowly destroyed. It was here, leaving my canoe in some bushes and climbing up the hill beneath the cover of thick trees and quickly falling darkness, that I stumbled upon them.

I watched from the shadows of the trees as a group of twenty-ish people huddled around someone I couldn't quite make out in the dark from behind. They stood before a structure, unmistakable against the last reds in the sky: a

short tower with a web-like network of thin
metal bars that matched Uncle M's sketch,
attached at its base to a disk of rubber and
metal. About an arm's length in diameter.
Sleek enough for a single person to drag down
a hill.

I saw a huge blue spark, accompanied by a
thunder-like crackle, cause the pile of logs to
go up in flames immediately, illuminating
everything. The gasping faces, the cable
running from the disk and tower to the flames,
and Oak, amidst the amazed faces of the
crowd in the light of the fire. He rose from the
ground, brushing dirt from his knees.

It wasn't prudence, at first, that kept me
from springing from the bushes, bounding
across the lawn, and throwing myself at him. I
was paralyzed. Here was the friend I'd
convinced myself was both dead and the
posthumous love of my life. Looking at him
now, I realized neither was true. I felt happy to
see him, but I didn't feel the urge to gallop
toward him, our mouths colliding a lifetime of
unrealized passion as I'd fantasized about in
my three days of solitude. In fact, I wasn't so
sure about kissing him, now; what would his
breath smell like after three days away from
the peppermint water of The Compound? My
eyes filled with tears of... what was it? Relief
that all was as it should be between us? Or

was it disappointment that I didn't feel that
burning ache for him that I'd felt when I'd
slept alone in his bed, played his guitar in the
dark, imagined his touch against mine? Then,
there was the question of these strangers; in
addition to Oak's audience, others milled
about, talking, rolling out mats, carrying
themselves with none of the aggression or
guardedness of others I'd seen around here.
Out here at The Archipelago, though, one
could never be too certain.

I waited until night fully fell, keeping my
eyes on Oak all the time, until I crept out into
the open field straight toward him, like I
belonged. I passed unnoticed. I'd had plenty of
practice as a ghost in the last few days.

He stood by the fire talking with two men,
their backs to me, and here is where I took the
risk, stepping fully into the fire's ring of light
and calling his name. All three figures turned
to me, the fire at their backs obscuring their
faces in the shadow. And just as the two men's
posture went defensive, legs back in unison
like leopards preparing to spring, Oak leapt at
me instead, his arms wrapping around my
neck and his legs wrapping around my waist in
a harmless embrace. I staggered back in the
grass with the weight of his affection, but I
didn't fall. The weight of his slender body was
familiar. He'd never been able to tackle me.

"I don't know how," he said into my ear in a low voice, "but I hoped you'd find me." He assured the others that I was a friend. He led me by the hand to the edge of the fire he'd sparked and sat in the grass with me. I'll admit his touch confused me, because it felt good and right, but also foreign. It was nothing like the powerful electricity I'd expect to feel if I were in love with someone. Then again, how would I know? It was, well... it was something. His touch made me nervous in a way it never had before.

He touched my elbow, and shoulder, and even my knee as he described sleeping under the stars in the company of these kind people, who'd found him at the shore curled around the base of the tower. It was a sort of ceasefire zone, where people came and went and shared their skills, scattering to personal hiding places about The Archipelago when storms came. It sounded nice, if a bit disorganized, notably less secure than The Compound. Finally, he came out with it:

"I feel wanted here. Needed. Like I have a lot to give."

I opened my mouth to protest, that he was *needed* at The Compound, and then I remembered what they did to him because of me. *We can always make more hands,* Uncle M had said. Then, I almost said that *I* wanted him, but truly I was confused. I'd convinced myself that I did want him, romantically, and then I'd seen him from the trees and decided I didn't, but then, here, in the firelight, with his fingertips brushing my knuckle, I didn't understand what I wanted. Still, I knew that I needed him.

So I said nothing. And he said nothing. And we looked at one another. And the fire popped and cracked.

"If you want to go back tomorrow," he said carefully, "you can take the tower. It's not good for much besides starting fires without anything to power up."

"If?" I repeated, not knowing what else to say. It was the first time I'd considered that as a serious option. Leave the safety of The Compound? For what? All my life, I'd been taught even pride and principal were laid down at the altar of the god of survival. On the other hand, how safe was it, really, for people like me, if Oak could be sent out to die after some secret agreement made in the shadows around the illuminated pages of a book some elders considered holy?

He pointed his smile toward the ground. "They might have a lot to learn from us both here."

God, if only he'd just say it. I got bold. One of us had to. "Is that what *you* want?"

He surprised me by reaching his hands forward and taking mine. "What I want is for you to stay here with us for a couple nights in the open air, under the stars. And then, we'll see what you want. What we both want. Unless you're in a big hurry to get back."

"Are you really going to stay here?"

"At least for a little while."

"What if they turn out to be just as bad as the folks at The Compound? Or worse?"

"Then we'll go somewhere else." He caught himself. "Or I will."

"Are you saying we'd be better off as nomads? The weather being what it is?"

"I'm not saying anything. Just that I might want to try. And maybe you might, too."

Oh, Oak. Believe it or not, this was him trying to be direct. I looked at our fingers interlaced, looked at his face, the Oak I knew, never one to confront something head-on. The Oak I knew, whose gestures of affection right now would get us *both* sent on a fool's errand of certain death back at The Compound. The Oak I knew, alive and well. The Oak I knew, but different. Freer. As if who he'd been at The Compound had been a mere ghost of his whole self. And he was still a mystery to me, Oak was. After my eternal three days of confinement poring over it, I'd expected everything to become clear if I found him alive. But I still had no idea whether he really had feelings for me, whether I even had feelings for him. I had no idea what parts of myself I'd have to better conceal for the safety of The Compound, let alone what parts of myself might come to light away from it. Would I like what I became? I didn't know. Couldn't. Nor did I know that anyone at The Compound would listen to me if I told them what had really happened, what had always been happening under our noses, who had been calling the shots in the name of our god of survival, our demi-god of safety, our supposedly sacred reverence for human life.

A hurricane had robbed me of that certainty, and a hurricane really did take Oak from me, too, in a way—it took the Oak I knew and replaced him with someone strange but not unfamiliar.

But what I did know? I knew that at The Compound, we'd tried the return to something like society, as it once was, and we'd seen what else had returned with it. I knew what it felt like in my belly to have Oak's hand in mine, here that whatever I decided I felt about Oak himself, I liked the thrill of *this* feeling well enough to want it more. So, I decided, well, I thought I could spare a couple nights here with him, under the stars. At the very least.

Blast & Brazen

By Astra Crompton

Erin Ballaster rounded the corner on Sparda and Fourth and tucked down a tight dead-end alley. The trick to not attracting civilian attention was to move forward with purpose; never shadily glance about.

At the end of the alley was her drop, right where Filter had said it would be.

<Found it?> crackled Filter in her earbud.

"If you're tracking me on GPS, why do you ask?" Erin whispered in reply, stripping out of her hoodie and jeans.

<Just being a friendly eye in the sky,> Filter answered as she swapped her Converse for a reinforced pair of sneakers, custom-built to withstand the kind of running Erin was capable of. Standing in her blue-and-black costume, she stuffed her discarded clothes and valuables into the drop—a small, featureless metal box—and heard it hiss as it sealed shut.

<I'll give you the passkey after the meeting,> Filter said in his usual chipper, digitally scrambled tone.

The meeting. Erin felt her mood sink as she scanned the street. Confirming no one was paying her any attention, she turned to face the nearest wall. It was too close to take it at a run, so she swung her arms in windmills, building up gyroscopic force in her core.

A moment later, static sparked all through her limbs with an audible crackle. Taking a step released a sudden explosive burst of speed; she zipped straight up the wall.

Spinning up over the rooftop in defiance of gravity, the city fanned out before her.

Another trick: never leave the way you entered. CCTV footage made vigilantism a delicate game.

As Erin sped across the skyline inside a fizzing ball of blue static, she tried to prepare herself to meet their latest recruit. Harrow had said this newest would-be hero was impervious to damage and super-strong. Filter had already run every background check and had no concerns.

Erin could picture him now: some macho, mansplaining dudebro who thought a balaclava counted as a costume and who would demonstrate his powers with a bench press. Besides, *another* man in the Waywards

wasn't her idea of "rounding out the team."
Aside from Consequence, Erin—or Blast, as
they called her—was the only other woman.

What had Harrow said Mr. Super-strong
was called?

Brazen. Of course it would be something
like Brazen. You could *hear* the bicep flex in
the first syllable.

<Turn off ahead,> crackled Filter.

"I see it," Erin answered, pitching herself
over the edge of an office building and
rocketing down between two columns of
windows towards the street. Feet still
sprinting, she tore down the subway stairs on
the corner. A boom of air broke behind her as
the pressure changed underground, but she
sped up the subway tunnel before the civilians
on the platform could react enough to cry out.

<Here!>

Erin skidded to a stop, digging a furrow
into the cement beside the track.

"Oops," she said.

<Not again! Can't you slow gradually?>
Filter asked.

"That was gradual. Nothing exploded, did
it?" she replied, as a metal service door
popped open on her right. Erin swung around
its frame, heard familiar chatter, and took a
deep breath.

"That is so *cool*!" Harrow's voice said, enthusiastic as ever.

"It sounds dangerous." A slight Nordic accent lilted Consequence's calm reply.

Erin padded into view, taking conscious steps so as not to bounce across the snug room.

"Blast, you made it!" Harrow cheered, waving one lanky arm at her from only a few feet away. His black mask made his skin look all the pastier, especially under the orange florescent service lights.

Behind him, a monitor flickered, spooling footage of Filter's goggles—all Erin had ever seen of his face. Consequence stood in the centre of the room, majestically tall, dressed in white, grey, and blood red. Mythos lounged against the far wall, swarthy in the shadows, his dark cape tucked into his crossed arms to cover the gauntlet that gave him his powers.

And then Erin saw the woman.

She was seated in a chair set up before Filter's screen, half-concealed behind Harrow. She looked Latina, a thick mass of curly hair pulled back from her brow by a bandana, wearing a fitted tank top and simple jeans. Heeled boots. A gold cross on a chain around her neck. No mask, no costume. She was beautifully buxom.

"Who's this?" Erin asked, staring at the stranger and enjoying it. A steady, brown-eyed gaze held hers. No curiosity, but plenty of assessment.

"Great question!" Harrow put out a hand, as if to touch the stranger, but stopped six inches away from contact. He could never touch her or anyone else. The Waywards all knew what would happen if he did. Harrow had promised, after the unfortunate Mythos-possession incident, that he would only use his disconcerting gifts on their opponents.

"Blast, this is Brazen. Brazen is thinking of joining up with the Waywards." Harrow grinned between them, as if introducing a friend to his mom for approval.

"*You're* Brazen?" Erin repeated.

"Yes," the brown-eyed goddess replied.

"Super-strong and invulnerable?" Erin asked.

Brazen stood up, shaking out her hands at her sides. "Go on, then," she said, her Cuban accent clearer with each word.

"What?" Erin asked, looking up at Brazen, then around at the others. Erin was easily the shortest one in the room—if one didn't count Filter's monitor height.

"Hit me, then." Brazen waited, calmly, gaze steady. "I'll prove it."

Pausing a moment to consider where best to strike, Erin swung her arm as if throwing a softball pitch, planting her fist squarely in Brazen's stomach. There was resistance, more like granite than flesh, but Brazen did not crumple. Instead, she skidded back a few feet, knocking into the workman's table and buckling its stainless-steel frame. She looked down at her boots, surprised.

"Ooooo-ee!" Harrow crowed, clapping loudly. "Brazen's *tough*. The first time you hit Mythos, he broke a wall."

"To be fair, I didn't know Blast was going to hit me, that time," Mythos grumbled from the far side of the room.

Consequence had approached at last and put out her hand, one of her red ribbons twined about her fingers. "May I?" she asked Brazen.

Brazen shrugged, looking back to Blast. There was curiosity in her expression now.

Consequence lifted the stranger's tank top to reveal perfect washboard abs, but no bruising, no damage. Nothing to show she's just taken the force of a truck to the guts.

"Can you feel this?" Consequence was asking, prodding Brazen's stomach.

"Feel what?" Brazen asked, looking down at last. "Oh. No, I told you. I can't feel anything."

"Nothing at all?" Mythos asked. "Not even a tickle from Blast?"

Brazen looked up. Her eyes searched Erin's face until Erin felt her cheeks flushing.

"No," Brazen answered, after a moment. "My body feels nothing."

"Well, I say she's in," Harrow announced. "Any seconds?"

"Yes!" Erin heard herself blurting. "Brazen can join us."

It wasn't until a week later, when Filter had put out the call that gang violence was wreaking havoc in Dunedin Square, that Erin truly appreciated why the newcomer was called "Brazen."

She was fearless.

Being invulnerable, Brazen simply walked into the fray between warring drug gangs. She gave no thought to the bullets rat-a-tatting against her, shredding her jeans and jacket. Nor to the knife one of the gang slammed up against her from behind. It was only the thug's surprised grunt as the blade broke that even alerted Brazen he was standing there.

She turned, implacable and statuesque, grabbed the boy by the throat, and tossed him into a dumpster without the slightest show of effort.

Erin was smitten.

As the Mustang's tyres squealed, its driver panicking to escape, Erin burst into action. She sprinted forward, her surrounding ball of static spun her across the square and around the vehicle in a wide arc. The driver let out an expletive and swerved. Erin planted her feet and punched with both fists: a shockwave exploded as her halted momentum burst. The passenger side of the car crunched beneath her force; the car rolled one-and-a-half times.

As the shattered glass sprayed across the concrete, Erin surveyed her team. All around, the rest of the Waywards were tackling the scattering gang members: the man carrying the duffle-bag of cocaine jerked about, handcuffing himself and the bag to a bike rack—Harrow's work; Mythos had pulled a green mace from his gauntlet's arsenal, and the weapon flung itself around the square, pummelling three, four, five of the gangsters; Consequence was keeping civilians away from the entrance into Dunedin Square. Erin evaluated where she could be of best help.

"Blast!"

She whipped around at Brazen's cry, and found the woman leaping to tackle her at the same moment she heard the gun fire.

The driver, of course. How could Erin have been so distracted?

But then Brazen's arms were clasped around her. The bear-hug was so extreme, one of Erin's ribs popped. She wheezed as the gun fired again, and again, until it clicked.

"Are you okay?" Brazen asked, peering down at her, a curl of her dark hair stuck to the wet of her lips.

"Ow?" Erin rasped, and Brazen's grip slackened at once.

"Sorry," she said, embarrassed, and turned away.

"No, I—" Erin lamely tried to clarify, but Brazen crossed the distance to the upturned car. The driver was struggling to reload while hanging upside-down from his seat. Brazen tapped the thug once on the forehead. His head snapped back, and he went slack, his seatbelt dangling him suspended.

"Wow," Erin said.

"You okay? Really?" Brazen called, already striding back into the square to help the other Waywards. "I can't tell, you know...how hard..."

"It's fine!" Erin offered a grin. "Thanks."

As Brazen nodded and turned away, Erin groaned at her own awkwardness. Shaking out her arms, she broke into a run again to snatch up a cluster of thugs running out the far-side of the square.

In the back of her mind, all she could think of was the warmth of Brazen's arms around her.

Two months later, while toweling off her hair after a fight, Erin's buzzer sounded. She padded barefoot across the laminate floor and hit the intercom button.

"Hello?" she said into its speaker.

"Hola, it's Miranda," came the voice through the static.

Erin's heartbeat stuttered. She didn't know anyone named Miranda but, despite the garbling of the intercom, the husky tone was unmistakable.

"Uh..." Erin said, and then realized she wasn't pressing the button. She hit it a little too forcefully; the plastic cracked and she cursed. "Hold on, just getting out of the shower," she said into the speaker.

The intercom crackled and half a word was cut off.

Erin scrambled for her earbud and stuffed it into place, hurrying as fast as she dared towards her bedroom to fetch bottoms and a shirt.

"Filter, is that Brazen?"

<At your apartment?> Filter answered at once. He never slept—*couldn't* sleep—and Erin

had gotten used to him being permanently On Call.

"Someone named Miranda is at my apartment," she hissed, though she wasn't sure why she was whispering. It wasn't as if she'd buzzed the visitor up. "Is that Brazen?"

<Yeah, her given name is Miranda. And yeah, security cams show her standing on your doorstep.>

"How did she find out where I live?" Erin demanded, kicking into her shorts and narrowly missing blowing a hole in the wall.

<I *may* have told her.> Filter's filter made his disguised voice screech up like a cartoon character.

"For crying out loud, why?" Erin demanded, shimmying into a t-shirt. She leaned to peer out the bedroom window before remembering her view was of the parking lot, not the front door.

<Who am I to stand in the way of romance?> Filter said.

Erin's heart threatened to strike.

"What?"

<Oh, come on! You *like* her.>

"That's none of your..." Erin began, her face heating up. The buzzer sounded again.

<At least go meet her downstairs. You don't have to invite her up.> Filter coaxed. <I didn't give her your unit number, or

anything.> Perhaps because he was agoraphobic and never met anyone in person, Filter felt playing with Erin's love life was an acceptable alternative. She tried to come up with a complaint, something to admonish him with, but her thoughts kept spiraling back to: I *do* like her.

Erin swept her short brown hair back behind her ears and padded back to the intercom.

With greater care, she squeezed the button and said, "Miranda? Come on up. It's 4112." She pushed the buzzer to unlock the front door and stepped away, hands sweating. Too late to take it back now. Filter's static in her ear sounded decidedly smug. She fished out the earbud and stuffed it into her shorts' pocket. Hastily she smoothed back her hair again.

She was still standing there, staring at the closed door, when it slammed in the frame. A muffled "*Dios mio!*" grumbled, and then two softer knocks sounded from the hall.

Erin wiped her sweating palms off on her shorts, then unlocked the door.

There she was: Brazen. Miranda. Dressed in an umber cowl-neck tunic-dress and black nylons, both of which clung to her every curve.

"Hello," Erin began, drinking in the sight of her.

"Hola," Miranda said again, offering a small smile. "Can I come in?"

"Yes, of course, yes!" Erin babbled, swinging back from the door to make way. As Miranda passed by her, Erin caught a whiff of perfume: something sweet yet spicy.

"Can I offer you a drink?" Erin asked, closing the door, and bolting it out of habit. "I've got water, tea...er, or water?"

The gorgeous woman turned around in the open main room of Erin's apartment. There wasn't much to look at: a sofa that was losing its shape on one side, from where Erin always curled up to read; a pair of standing lamps on extension cords; a small television and PVR box on a refurbished dresser, painted electric blue; a single plush circular carpet in the middle of the floor; and a couple of side tables where she kept keys, spare change, her iPod, unopened mail, Aspirin, and a small cactus named Ringo.

"Black tea?" Miranda asked, coming to a stop facing her.

"Can be," Erin replied, trying to move into the kitchen without taking her eyes off the way the lamplight glistened in Miranda's dark curls, made all the brighter by the orange of her dress. "No milk, no sugar?"

"Black as it gets, please," Miranda answered.

"Sure," Erin said. "Feel free to have a seat."

Erin watched as Miranda took steady steps across the laminate flooring, the *click-clack* of her heels a sounding board so she could judge her weight and force. She paused before the sofa, subtly measuring the distance with her arm before turning around and sitting carefully. She paused for a moment, arms bent at her sides, and then relaxed. She sank into the battered upholstery.

Erin ducked back into the kitchen lest her guest think she was spying on her. As she put the kettle on to boil, Erin called out, "So... You can taste black tea?"

"Yes, I can taste things in general," Miranda called back.

"I wasn't sure how it worked," Erin said by way of apology. "Have you always been, well, invulnerable?"

"Ever since I can remember. When I was little, my parents thought it was leprosy. But, they take me to the doctor, and they do tests, and no leprosy. I get older, they do more tests, for nerves, this time, and that is how they find out I am...Superdotado."

"'Dotado'? You mean Gifted?" Erin asked, leaning against the doorway into the kitchen as she listened for the kettle.

"Gifted, yes," Miranda repeated. "My Abuela arranged for an exorcism, and when that didn't work, she sent me to live with my aunt here."

"Woah," Erin said without thinking. "Like, a young priest and an old priest—the whole bit?"

Miranda stared at her, her expression confused, but nodded. "Yes, with a priest. It was not nice."

A beat of awkward silence passed between them as Erin tried to think of something to say. In the end, she just turned back into the kitchen to grab the kettle off its element and poured the scalding water into her teapot, its ceramic the same cornflower blue as her eyes.

"So, you can't feel pain," she called again, after a moment. "What about heat? Cold?" *Pleasure,* she wondered, but couldn't bring herself to ask. What would life be like if you couldn't feel *anything?*

"No..." Miranda trailed as Erin re-emerged from the kitchen carrying the teapot. A couple of mismatched mugs hung by their handles from her fingers. "I can't burn, but I do sweat. My teeth rattle when it's cold," Miranda finished.

"Chatter, you mean?"

Miranda gave a slightly sheepish smile and shrugged. "Probably that's what I mean."

Erin nearly had the opposite problem, where she had to hone her sensitivity to prevent herself from blasting holes in things when she only meant to touch them. It wasn't that she was super-strong, like Brazen, it was that she built up compounded force. Without her gyroscopic ball of static, Erin was as vulnerable as the next person. Sure, stubbing her toe a year ago had meant needing to replace the whole bathtub, but it had still *hurt.*

Erin set the mugs down, one white with a silhouette figure in fast sprint and the words RUN LIKE ZOMBIES ARE CHASING YOU, and another pale green one with little yellow and blue cacti printed on it.

"Which one do you want?" Erin asked, gesturing to the mugs, and checking on the steep of the tea.

Miranda inspected both, smiled at the running one but pushed it towards Erin.

"That one belongs with you. I will take the cactus, thank you."

Erin poured out tea into both, leaving room in her own for a bit of sugar. As she stirred it in, she finally sat on the other side of the couch, instinctively folding one lean leg under herself.

"So, what can I do for you?" Erin asked.

Miranda lifted the mug in both hands, staring at the tea as she pressed her lips to the rim and took a mouthful. After setting the steaming mug back onto the table with a click, Miranda pushed a hand back into her curls, propping her elbow on the back of the couch to lean towards Erin.

"Maybe, I think you can tell me where to get a proper...máscara."

Erin blinked, looking at Miranda's fresh face, only a bit of lipstick on her full mouth. Her dark lashes framed her eyes perfectly.

"I don't think you need any make-up," Erin replied a little hesitantly. "And I'm not much of a make-up girl. For beauty tips, you'd best ask Consequence."

"Beauty? No, I mean your—*cómo se dice?*" She mimed covering her eyes.

"Oh! Mask!" Erin laughed despite herself, nearly spilling her tea. "My costume?"

"Yes, Blast and Harrow and Mythos—all have these costume. I think I will stay with the Waywards for a long time, so I too should have good costume."

Erin continued to smile, loving listening to her accent and the earnest way Miranda made eye-contact as if she could transmute her meaning even if words failed her. There was a heartbeat or two of silence before Erin realized she was supposed to answer. She looked away, flushing.

"Well, for that, you'll have to ask Filter. He hooked us all up with these suits. Knowing him, he probably already has something in mind for you. He likes to plan ahead." She picked up her own mug and sipped, imagining their mysterious recon specialist fizzing smug static somewhere.

"And Blast? You too like to plan ahead?"

Erin blinked, glancing back to this bronzed goddess leaning on her shabby sofa, and her heart leapt into her throat. There was something intimate in the way Miranda said it, something searching, and Erin desperately wanted to be found.

"My name is Erin," she said at last. "Blast is just my alias."

"Erin," Miranda repeated, smiling too. "I like this. Thank you."

After that, the conversation developed its flow. They talked about their respective Gifts, and about how they both got into fighting hoodlums. There always seemed to be a drug dealer or a mugger in every origin story. Despite different beginnings, different languages, different ages—Miranda was a good seven years older than Erin—they had the same secret to bind them together.

It was the first time Erin had been able to chat up a girl that she could be fully honest with. In a life of lies about who she was or where she had been or why she was bruised, honesty was intoxicating.

As the evening grew later and the teapot became cold and empty, Erin found herself leaning against the back of the couch. Her cheek rested on one forearm as she smiled at Miranda, who mimicked her posture only scant few inches away.

"So, you've never been kissed," Erin said, staring at Miranda's mouth as if hypnotized.

"No, I *have* been kissed," Miranda countered. "A boy named Xavier who lived next door to my Abuela. When I was ten."

"Oh," Erin replied, her buoyancy deflating a little. Perhaps Miranda only liked men. She was Catholic, after all.

Miranda shrugged. "I wasn't impressed. I didn't feel the spark, as you say."

Erin saw Miranda crack a smile and grinned in reply, feeling suddenly shy. "So, I guess it's not something you want, then. Or need."

"No, of course I *want* it. It is so frustrating to want and know I can never have love." Miranda sighed, her gaze growing wistful, and she reached out to press a strand of Erin's bangs behind her ear.

Sparks shot up Erin's spine, and suddenly she was completely alert. The touch had been clumsy; Miranda's short fingernail caught on the conch of her ear unpleasantly before managing to tuck her hair in place, but Erin's balloon of hope rocketed for the ceiling.

"If you can't feel touch, how would you..." Erin trailed. Even though this was the one woman Erin's compounding force wouldn't hurt, there didn't seem much point if Miranda got nothing out of it.

"I told you," Miranda answered slowly, her smile becoming wry. "I can sweat. I can taste and see." She paused, sitting up and pushing her curls back over her shoulder. "I confess: You remember the driver with the gun?"

Erin nodded, sitting up as well. She clasped her hands against her ankle as if holding on to a roller coaster's safety bar.

"When I hold you in my arms then, and you smell like...electricity? I have thought of that many nights. If you let me hold you again, so that you are close, I promise to be careful."

Erin sat in slack shock as Miranda's dark eyes searched her face. Then, slowly Erin smiled. She slid carefully across the few inches remaining between them and pulled herself into Miranda's lap. She didn't need to worry about accidentally knocking her knee against Miranda's or about yanking her hair as a thick curl got trapped between their arms. Erin made every gesture deliberately so that Miranda could imagine what it might feel like.

She wrapped her arms around Miranda's neck and tucked in close. Miranda took a deep breath and let out a contented sigh.

They sat like that for uncountable minutes. Erin listened to Miranda's pulse pattering an excitable jazz rhythm and tried to process never knowing touch. No mother's hug, no scraped knees, no wind in your hair—and no kisses.

"Miranda?" Erin murmured, mouth brushing Miranda's firm throat. "Would you let me love you? We can use your other senses, in ways. Scent and sound and so on."

Miranda's arms squeezed, but not painfully this time. "Yes," she whispered back. "I think this is why I come here, after all."

Craning her neck back, Erin tried to copy Brazen's playbook and let go of her fear. She kissed Miranda's full mouth, luscious yet unresponsive, except for the squeeze of Miranda's hand on her waist and the warmth in her eyes.

For all their Gifts, Blast and Brazen were two imperfect beings trying to make each other whole. They didn't need costumes or exorcists or even the same senses to truly understand one another. They fit together perfectly, and love was something found in the space between.

Jennifer

Richard Leise

Jennifer did not go by Jen, and she certainly did not answer to Jenny. Her name was like her face, a sensible organization of set, or fixed, shapes. Her name was not a haircut, a style, some part of herself that, for wedding or whim, could be cut, fashioned, washed, or rinsed, simply to, whenever she cared, grow back out, rework, restore, if not quite resurrect, to attain some semblance of its former self. There were no nicknames. There was no unique spelling. Her name was non-negotiable. Jennifer. Two Ns. That was it.

Some people, maybe even most, did not get this. Jennifer did not mind. There are certain things, perhaps the most important things, that matter. And if no one else understands? Well, Jennifer could not care less. She thought about this often, carefully, and deliberately, never conflating conviction with desire, or

fancy, or with what her mother called "whim."
In this way, life passed by. And then Jennifer
met Jennifer.

She was sitting in front of Hannah Mills,
right there on the sidewalk, drawing. Jennifer
had made for the building because she had
nothing better to do. About four blocks from
campus, the structure was listed on the
National Register of Historical Places. Jennifer
didn't know why the building had been given
the designation. A couple of minutes online
revealed nothing, other than some general
platitudes. The few Hannah Mills links were
redundant, absent substance, like emails from
her mom, emotional spam. With a Cntl + alt +
delete Jennifer grabbed her phone, wallet, and
sunglasses, chewed what remained of her
lollipop, slid its white plastic handle inside a
Snickers wrapper, and locked her office. She
tossed her trash in a can by the elevator.

Shadows masked rooftops. Modified
sunlight—Jennifer wore Oliver Peoples—made
particularly black the thorns detailing the
trunks of the honey locust planted between,
and around, the university's tall, brick,
buildings. Made iridescent red and blood
orange were those legumes shriveling
between the tree's pretty yellow leaves, leaves
in pattern alternate and spiral, a calliope of
color.

The lollipop was legit. Morphine was a wonderful drug. Jennifer loved the high. How it got her to feeling totally unnecessary. She registered the desert heat as something interesting. It constantly amazed, being here. Away from water—let alone three rivers—and the smell of fallen industry. Buildings, undoubtedly made of steel, looked like solid-earth constructions, as if carved from the land. Even the people—comprised of the same body parts of those back east—looked different. Assembled not so much from length or limb but shaped, contoured, by those concurrent winds comprising her own escape. She noticed that she was smiling. But to other thoughts Jennifer claimed a sort of animalistic purchase. Chiefly, she summoned those judgments concerning command, knowing, without thinking, that encapsulated within these sentiments—like powder within pills— were precise degrees of clarity. When electing to forego direct insight (if she had popped and was running Apache, or if she had smoked some Dust) Jennifer operated from a carefully cultivated certainty. What she did was right because it was right. She did not suffer from doubt.

There were many people around. Her eyes were hidden. Concealed. Her black hair, even when pulled into a ponytail with a green rubber band, was pretty. She looked wealthy, sexy, not gay, and certainly not queer. Like the Founding Fathers, she held certain truths to be self-evident.

Jennifer loved fashion, and she knew that she looked way more Portia de Rossi than Ellen DeGeneres. (Not that there was anything wrong with this.) Her beauty was a source of amusement and frustration. Envy eluded her, as did spite. Jennifer knew she should feel less human, but because she didn't experience guilt, this aspect of her condition was a bit confusing. Which was to say that none of this came as a relief. These facets of her character probably added, rather than subtracted, from her personality. Either way, it didn't matter. When her mom emailed and asked if she was dating, or if she had a boyfriend, she replied, "You're kidding?"

Regarding influence, wide, given that she understood life to be one hundred percent performance, was Jennifer's particular sphere. The thing was, though, she wasn't acting. She was the Other. They—whomever they were— didn't understand her. You'd have thought this was why Jennifer became a geneticist. You'd have been wrong. Erasing this ambiguity was not particularly interesting. Creating a universal sort of understanding wasn't even appealing.

It had been Jennifer's experience that bigots weren't, generally speaking, terrible people. They were just ignorant. Raised dumb. Jennifer liked visiting the nearby pond. She felt for the ducks with the broken legs, and fully realized empathy for those geese that, because of some whacked-winged defect, were never—ever—going to get that tossed piece of bread. You had no control over how you were born, and, in a way, you had less control as to how you were raised. If science could tell her 'how' she was gay, who cared? What did it matter? Jennifer didn't believe that anyone wanted a cure for homosexuality. Not really. Gay people were happy. And people for whom homosexuality was a sin? Well, they would have one less cause for which to pray. And people who prayed, at least Jennifer's mom, and her pious circle of friends, would be bothered by this disruption. These women weren't exactly Plato, but they did think in universals. And what else was there to pray for, really, aside from peace (this encompassed the oppressed) and the sick (that covered your dead and starving) and the homosexuals (which took care of depravity)? Bigots (who, really, weren't much different than those broken ducks), were going to marry idiotic women and raise idiotic children. Within their homes these unnecessary families, sitting upon furry sofas itchy with dog dander, alternating between boredom and the pleasure of watching TV—like broken Buddhas, enlightenment arriving when accidentally entering the heady torpor of pleasant boredom—would, without effort, complete God's, or Whoever's, plan. But this, of course, had only been Jennifer's experience.

When she was fourteen, a few boys in their church had been molested by Father Simon. Jennifer's mother had explained that while most men prefer women as their sexual partners, some others, even good men, like Father Simon, prefer men. She said that there was even a word for it, that these men are called homosexuals. Had she heard that word, her mother wanted to know? Homo. Sexual?

Had Jennifer been twelve, instead of fourteen, her mother would have been crying. But Jennifer's mother had quickly accepted Jennifer's radical daughter-cum-teenager ascension. She learned that to cry was to undermine her credibility as authority, and that, like a wild animal, her daughter detected weakness. And so she delivered the facts of life as if at church, reading Ezekiel from the lectern. What Jennifer wanted to learn was what made Father Simon homosexual. Because the consensus, even if only posed as questions by her mother's friends, was that something must have happened. Why else would such an otherwise nice and intelligent man be that way?

What Jennifer's mother refused to reveal, Jennifer discovered online. Here, clear-headed, she unlearned all that her mother had told her. Unpolluted, inhaling, like face drugs, air ancient and non-toxic, untouched by some city's strings of smoggy tentacles, generated her own worldview. Predicated upon this point-and-click milieu, Jennifer's perspective evolved wildly. In time, the sound of fingers upon keyboards struck her as symphonic, compositional in nature, as music arriving from some other place. Jennifer didn't believe in aliens. Were there, Jennifer's opinion was that they were far more likely to have invented the Internet than to have given us the Pyramids.

Here is something Jennifer read, and retained. It had been debated for a long time whether a person's sexual preference is innate, learned, or due to a combination of both causes. One article—it is still available, just go to your favorite search engine and type "Klar"—claimed that the human right-versus-left-hand use preference and the direction of scalp hair-whorl rotation develop from a common genetic mechanism. Such a mechanism, the scientist argued, controls

functional specialization of brain hemispheres.
Whether the same mechanism specifying
mental makeup influences sexual preference
was determined by comparing hair-whorl
rotation in control groups supplemented with
homosexual men with that in males at large.
Without getting too specific, there were
experiments. Results suggested that sexual
preference may be influenced in a significant
proportion of homosexual men by a biological /
genetic factor that also controls the direction
of hair-whorl rotation. Jennifer's takeaway:
According to Klar, if you take a close look at
the back of the head of the guy giving you
head, there is a thirty percent chance that he's
gay.

But still. Cynicism aside. Say this was true.
Jennifer couldn't see how knowing this would
help anyone other than—*maybe*—someone
uncomfortable with her sexuality. Just because
you could explain gay didn't mean a bigot
would care any less. Didn't people who hated
Jews know what made them Jewish? And if
they didn't. Did it matter? And if white people
didn't get how they were different from Black
people? Well, and Jennifer slowed, she stopped
walking, those poor suckers were even
dumber than she gave them credit for. Jennifer
knew that she could no more heal a bigot than

her mom could name more than one continent. And Jennifer was okay with that.

At the north end of campus, a group of buildings rose to great heights. Parking garages with gaping apertures and education buildings with mirrored windows distended like huge chunks of coral amber and umber, creating a sort of urban reef, strange forms rising from this petrified ocean floor. Recent additions, they served to make Jennifer feel both tall and small, a piece of cake in one hand, a mushroom in the other. She moved on.

Jennifer waited to cross Virginia Ave. She wasn't in a hurry. Her legs tingled. Relaxed, her shoulders lifted, a light, muscular release. The light regulating the intersection yellowed. Or maybe it was green. Jennifer could never remember when she was permitted, legally, to cross the street. Cars passed slowly by.

Hannah Mills, a block away, was large enough to see. Built primarily in the Greek Revival Style, and this upon a sacred Acoma burial site, its façade, comprised of four huge, carved columns rising from marble bases, supported the stoa. Seventy feet high, stone walls several feet thick housed a couple hundred rooms, bathrooms, offices, and wide hallways. The mid-interior, made visible through two huge street level glass doors,

featured impressive arched stairs. Shadows
made the building seem blue.

Sitting in front of the building, right there
on the sidewalk, a pretty girl drew a picture.
Jennifer appraised her. Flats off to the side,
her feet, toenails painted indigo, were flush
with the concrete. Her raised knees created an
easel. Jennifer understood that she should be
startled (she had not noticed the girl until just
now) and processed the realization. The girl
was not drawing the building, but what looked
like a woman. The woman appeared to be
kneeling upon the bottom of the ocean, a wet,
snuff-colored desert behind, and off to either
side of her. Her eyes were huge, her pupils
were expanded—and this so dramatically to
have done away with iris, with sclera—just a
bit of opaqueness, rendered, through
incredible technique, viscous. One-third of her
face was hidden, eaten, consumed by the outer
darkness. Clearly visible was the outline of a
skull, a neon sort of band red rolling to fuse
with her neck and which fell, unmistakably,
into a shoulder. And this—now orange—rolling
to define her back, which, luminous, rounded
to inform her rear end. From the curve of her
shoulder two brilliant yellow lines descended
at a bit of an angle, perfectly vertically. This
was an arm, terminating in nothing. This
meant that the woman didn't have hands. Or,

maybe, and Jennifer angled her head, that the woman's hands were dug into the sand.

"So...what do you think?" the girl said. She sang the question.

Jennifer, slow to give her opinion, even to people she knew, said, "It's wonderful. I mean—" And Jennifer raised her sunglasses.

In looking down upon the picture it was as though the woman flickered. Not like a broken bulb. No, it was more as though she, the woman, was the faulty socket. Jennifer made out that the figure's arm was in front of a knee. Clear, the deep-green outline of her thigh. Her hamstring. And her knee, which rounded at its cap .... Here began, or was so concentrated, a thick, dull, blue, which intensified to mark her abdomen. Clearly tone, this rose to swell, a sort of violet outlining the heft of a considerable breast. This—her chest—was, of course, incredibly buoyant. Jennifer lowered her shades. She said, "It's amazing."

"What, are you some sort of activist or something?" The girl looked up and shielded her eyes. She lowered her hand when realizing there wasn't a glare. She resembled *Pulp Fiction* Uma Thurman. Her chest pressed against her thin cotton t-shirt.

"Are you an artist?"

"If you mean, 'Am I queer?' the answer to that," and the girl placed her pad and pastels to the side, wiped her hands on her jeans, slipped on her flats, and stood, dusting her rear end, "is yes. Want to know what I think? Nice shades, by the way."

Jennifer didn't know what to say.

"It's pretty. Symmetric, but not ostentatious. Sober, and evenly balanced. Like a ballerina. Assuming," and she smiled, "that buildings can be anthropomorphized. Other than that," and she frowned, she crossed her arms, "I think it's fucked."

"Fucked?"

"Yeah. They put it on top of some Indian burial ground, which is fine, I guess, if you didn't know it. I mean all of this," and she moved a hand above her head. "All this is built upon something sacred. To someone. Just cause it's the United States doesn't mean it's not a continent. People lose sight of this. All of this. So, we're like, just by doing anything, going to sully everything. But once you find out that shit—Hey, wait," and the girl turned. "Don't make me an idiot. Am I telling you stuff you already know?"

Jennifer shook her head. She couldn't speak. Cotton mouth. Sure. But there was more to that than this. Weren't they talking about the drawing?

"Then why are you here?"

Jennifer explained.

"Oh. Right. Yeah. That. Why didn't you just look online? But that's dumb, though. You're right. Nothing there. You look like a professor, but not history?"

Jennifer said that she was, and that she wasn't.

"You're definitely not from here. This," and she waved her hand in the air. "This area. The region. You're too yellow for that. And it's not L.A. Let me guess." The girl gave it some thought. "Philly."

Jennifer shook her head; she didn't know what to say. So, she said, "No. Pittsburgh."

"Close enough. Same state. Gross. Sorry."

"It's not that bad. I mean, it wasn't always, anyways."

Satisfied, the girl continued. "Thought so. There's a historical marker over there," and she pointed to a side of the building. "But it's nothing. Before all the dead Indian controversy, the place is just old, for the U.S. anyways, and it's been, whatever, brick-by-brick transplanted here from somewhere in New York—not New England, don't believe what you read—and supposedly Mark Twain wrote some story about a frog in it. Or maybe it was a catfish? Although I could be wrong about that. The frog part." She stooped to

gather her materials and slid them into a
portfolio. "Or the catfish, I guess. Pretty sure
the bit about Mark Twain is true. Anyways,
rich people, Hannah Mills, whoever the frog
that is, or her family, moved it here for some
reason or other. Something something Hudson
River Boston. Dunno. The fucked part is that
there was a water break in the basement? And
once the water, like, dissipated? They found all
these human remains. And apparently some
sort of shield. Really rare, really cool stuff. Our
version of antiquity, right? Here, check this
out."

She leaned into Jennifer. So close that
their foreheads touched, that their hair
intertwined. The smell was like fresh air.
Jennifer's stomach swirled. Immediately
horny, she was also high, and so she simply
shuddered.

"Can you see?"

"What am I looking at?" Jennifer said. She
moved closer, rested so that her forearm
brushed the girl's chest.

"Right?" the girl said. She set her art
supplies on the sidewalk, between her feet,
and cupped the phone like a chalice. "That's
called a ewer. No one really knows, or those
who know aren't saying, more likely," and she
rested a temple against Jennifer's. "But the
word is that it's at least a thousand years old,

and that it's not Indian. Like, U.S. Indian. It could be from India, for all I know. But it's not Native American, is what I'm saying."

Jennifer studied the picture. The ewer—which looked like a jar, the sort genies came from—was beautiful. Clearly dirty, the glass was still bright, glowing a sort of—

"It's like it's glowing," Jennifer said.

"Right?"

"And not orange, but more," she turned her head, felt her face brush the girl's—

"Tangerine."

"Yeah," Jennifer smiled. "Exactly. Tangerine. It's so cool. Wait," and she leaned towards the image.

"Is there something inside there?" she added.

"Sure does seem like it, doesn't it," the girl said, pocketing her phone. "But we'll never know. Instead of doing the right thing, like, say, listening to the Indians? The site, though no one admits this, is currently under excavation. And you know what else?"

Jennifer didn't.

"You know that show *Ghost Stories*?"

The girl had raised an arm to shoulder her supplies, exposing a muscular stomach that angled into the lace edge lining her panties.

"That a no? Well, it's pretty dumb, but it's fun. It's on Fridays, at least the new ones,

anyways. Anyways, permits and production are
in place to film from the site, directly. Next
week, I think. I saw the host on campus the
other day. Dresses like a mannequin from Hot
Topic? Almost like he's trying for silly, but,
since he's not, it's embarrassing? He was
trying to get something for free? Like a bagel,
or something? Such bullshit. Not the bagel
thing."

The girl started walking, and Jennifer
stepped beside her. Their shadows, flung
before them, angled, they merged to become
one.

"Although that's pretty gay, too. But after
they film their show, tenured archeologists
from EU, and a select, hand-picked core of
'world-renowned' peers are pooling resources
under the pretense of an 'Unwavering
dedication to the natural world and those who
inhabit it,' and they're going to dig up and
dust off body parts and burial goods. The
beards, depending upon perceived value, are
then going to "re" everything. Repatriate,
rebury, rebuke, reproach, in some fucking
manner relocate every sherd and castellation,
every skull and cast, all the while developing
"protocols" to guide those who wish to
conduct additional archeological research,
both in Endwell and elsewhere, ensuring that
human remains and cultural artifacts similarly

related from this area don't end up like the
Hebron, or some such tribe. Can't remember
which one. Read about it, sure. But that
doesn't mean I get what any of it means."

Hot and uncomfortable, Uma readjusted
her supplies. Jennifer had no interest in
carrying anything, and didn't offer to help. It
wasn't that she didn't care about people, it
was that she liked sweating, less. Plus, the
math worked. At least one of them would not
be hot and uncomfortable.

And then, "The point the professors and all
them are trying to make is that all of the
artifacts are being treated with the care and
the respect they deserve, that they're not
subject to abuse by pot-hunters, or that they
end up in Endwell Antiques. You know the
mayor?"

Jennifer did not.

"That a yes? Well, according to Mr. Mayor,
the plan is to cultivate some sort of field
school that's going to emphasize respect and
spiritual consciousness. This, apparently, in
addition to scientific technique. He even used
the word 'woke.' But incorrectly." Uma
laughed. "Such a tool."

Jennifer did not know how to use woke,
either. She associated the word with the NBA.
She loved the NBA, particularly post-game
press conferences, where her favorite players,

dressed for the catwalk, fielded questions from reporters. She wanted to be a reporter. How much fun it would be to craft such pointless questions, and to pose them with such solemnity, and this while already knowing the coming answer. She said, "How do you know all this?"

"A friend edits *The Endwell Standard*."

"*The Endwell Standard*?"

Uma laughed. "Oh man, this place really is pathetic. You. A tenured, I presume, professor. You've never heard of *The Standard*?"

Jennifer shrugged.

The sun was setting. It was not night, but it was getting there. There was a warm breeze. Soon, the campus would be erased, reduced to a series of stark, simple shapes, black against the austere rise of the blacker hillsides, miles away. Atop one of these four broadcast masts. And the masts descended in height, like a set of Russian Dolls. There were four aircraft warning lights positioned evenly upon each mast. And these lights were red. And these red lights blinked idly. These red lights blinked slowly. And then an interrupted darkness. Above the sidewalks and above the sidelines of athletic fields iridescent rape lights sparkled bug-zapper blue. Light posts illuminated empty roads, and light from square bulbs framed empty parking lots, an iridescence, each, poking and prodding at nature. From her office Jennifer would watch them glittering fantastically, some of them like collapsing stars blinking on and then off, on and then off again, a patterned permanency erased only by the risen sun.

Presently, though, Endwell began to gloam. Not quite bright with twilight, and not yet disrupted by dark, the air was thick with asphalt and exhaust, the Cimmerian sky impossible, the sky, like good thoughts dissolving into other good thoughts, vacated by its own nothingness. The sun was in the west. It was hot. Around Uma a sort of approximated sunlight. Atop the asphalt the appearance of waves. Look a bit further in the distance, let loose your eyes, and these waves assume greater clarity. Because Jennifer knew the waves for what they were, she did not see them as chimera, or mirage, but a form of heat, something abstract made concrete. A jet soundlessly traced a seam in the sky, its contrail dissipating in bands like splatter paint.

"I don't live far," Uma said. "Wanna go listen to some records? Maybe brush up on some *Standard*? Do the whole formal introductions? I'm Jennifer, by the way."

The sexual orientation of a fruit fly can be genetically programmed. This is a scientific fact. Neurobiologists have discovered that homosexuality, in fruit flies, can be turned on or off. If you give a fruit fly a certain drug—Jennifer cannot remember which—it changes the way the insect's sensory circuits react to pheromones.

Jennifer prayed that Uma was not bi.

Literally, as they walked a couple blocks further from campus, closer to the pubs and bars, Jennifer thought through four Hail Mary's, and she was most of the way through the Act of Contrition when Uma, after taking Jennifer's hand, led her across the street. She unlocked the door leading to her apartment.

Of course, the obvious was acknowledged, and the Jennifers smiled. How funny. This was early, sex and sweat, together, always together, naked in bed. Jennifer's condo was on the fifth floor, about five miles from campus, and through her bedroom window a barren wilderness, but not always. There were no trees, but every spring this wasteland blossoming, every April from the ground a rainbow of color rising, the desert's wide array of succulents and cacti, of wildflowers and grasses, and all of it glossed—the yellow flowers atop the Barrel Cactus, the bluish-greens of the Juniper's seedlings, the plump, globular reds of the Desert Christmas Cactus, the gray sheen of the of the rising Century Plant's basal rosette—all of it was altered by a sort of sun-soaked, feverish ocher, the white-washed glow of some mad impressionist's dream. But briefly. Then the sun came even closer and melted every yellow petal and ruined every blue berry and fried the red flowers and made leather those evergreens.

Were there trees, the trees would make outside the window a foreground where otherwise there is nothing, where otherwise there is just that unnamed distance, the flesh of the surrounding desert, the wind-blown dunes, the rise and fall of the low-lying hillsides, and these hillsides dipped in shadow, the desert from which they rise rich with darkness and undulating definition and not without beauty but this beauty of a quiet sort, capable, as if a painting, of evoking something bucolic, some sense of the rolling pasture touched with the dusty drab of dusk. Later, much later, after the sun has completed its arc, after the sun has set below the hillside, color spreads across the horizon. Like a flame alighting a bed of coals, these low-lying hillsides in outline. Electric blue. Deep purple and pink. And this color fading, the sky assuming, like grains of sand in some mystic mandala, shades orange and yellow and turquoise green before yielding to evening's celestial blue, distant stars poking through this federal firmament bright as stars.

Oh, how we take so much for granted! And this whether it is something that we grab, or be it something we have been given. Jennifer—who is about to become Fern—will not feel bettered. Fern will not feel beaten. The contest that Fern—then Jennifer—accidentally entered? Ineffable. (And so No. I will not complain. I will not protest. I will not claim I was cheated. I lost, Fern thinks.)

Still, though, and Fern brought a hand to her mouth. What is about to happen is nothing you shake off. Some days (and today is one of them) Fern will open her eyes and the world will seem a little too bright. Acute, the feeling that that she will one day die, offset by the certainty that she is healthy, that she is going to lead a long life. This is melancholy. Home alone (because Jennifer is out there somewhere, being Jennifer) Fern will leave for work, and the drugs won't work, and of course she will feel the heat, and she will associate this heat with the sunshine, but, if you were to ask, Fern would only raise a hand and point to the heavy, stolid weight of the power lines. This is not melodrama. Fern will not want to get hit by a drunk driver, but she would not report one, either. On the drive home she will not listen to Beach House. In the shower she will not think of Franziska Michor. God's honest truth, she will email her mother.

For the first month the Jennifers interacted only with each other, so the fact that they shared a name meant nothing. What Jennifer (now Fern) did not know, had no way to know, was that Jennifer, the first person to truly get her, a woman not only sexy and beautiful but smart, funny, and legitimately—and this as in immensely—talented, would no more forgo her name than she would sew closed her vagina. Comparatively, Jennifer (now Fern) only liked her name, and this only because it was hers, because it was a given. Relative to Jennifer's obsession, Fern (then Jennifer) could only be said to possess a strong preference. An artist, Jennifer did not think of her name in metaphor. She certainly did not think of her name in abstract. (Or, even lamer, Fern flushed at the thought, she did not draw some parallel with her mother.) Her Jennifer was a noun, concrete. Jennifer was Jennifer, and savagely. By the time Fern (then Jennifer) came to this realization, it was too late. She was in love.

Early in what prove to be serious, life-long relationships, one large row, as opposed to a string of petty, juvenile arguments, an event perhaps predictable if not exactly forecasted, positions rather than pure emotions like two fronts colliding and creating not so much the storm, but the lightning strike which starts the wildfire, and to the degree that there is destruction this sort of fight—which, arising from a different sort of nature, develops naturally—lays waste to the forest, making it not so much possible to see through the trees as eviscerating them, creating the necessary ground upon which the seeds of something fresh are free to shoot, the roots in such soil spreading and taking hold, clutching something new, and presumably stronger, this relationship, before undefined, now given the space to grow, that room necessary to go about the business of establishing those boundaries demarcating an exclusive relationship. While not necessarily the sort of conflict that cemented such a relationship— enough had already transpired between the Jennifers to convince the couple that they were going to be together, and forever—this fight, contingent upon the combatant, could easily have been the sort to end it.

As far as causality was concerned, their fight, insomuch as root cause was concerned, was perfect. Serious enough to matter, and deeply, to both. And so significant that both Jennifers were able to understand, and empathize with, the other's position. What made the concern particularly potent—up there with, say, placing one's career over another's, or agreeing to move away from family—was that, once resolved, someone was going to end up doing nothing but receiving. While the other would be left with nothing at all.

Neither wanted to admit how much her name mattered. To do so was to confess. To do so was to lower her defense, and, in a way, seek absolution. There is duality. Only Aquinas had it wrong. The soul is corruptible. The Jennifers believed in Foucault. The soul imprisons the body. To expose not just a part of yourself, but the very essence of yourself? It is their spirits, it has been their souls which have been created to be fortified, to be strengthened by a resolve to protect this self, this body corporeal, from those elements both internal and external, forces both within and without, those Others intent upon shaping them into some lesser being. Into some Other.

At their cores were shared positions with regard to topics as incendiary as abortion (the Jennifers were pro-life), and as polarizing as polygamy (when so much of the country was quick to marry, only to divorce, who said the West had it right?), the Jennifers, in being queer, did not believe that being feminist was a requirement. Jennifer was a scientist. Her sexuality afforded her a unique insight into the prevailing literature—interestingly, she ripped online headlines, heavily couched them with ideas harvested from Puritan sermons (she particularly enjoyed the skewed syntax)—and published widely. Her classes, while never full, were never empty. Admired more than she was liked, Jennifer (before she became Fern) attracted grad students who, bright, but, intellectually, terrifically average, loved living vicariously the life of an academic. They emulated Jennifer, and, doing their best to dress fashionably, paced the hallways outside her office, laptops open, pining, when not in one of her classes, for proximity. She had them TA. She let them grade papers. Only their coffees gave them away. Jennifer (still Jennifer) did not do caffeine. Pretty much anything but caffeine. When asked if she would get them to sit for a painting, Jennifer (still Jennifer) said, "Ha."

A painter, Jennifer's work sold in Paris and New York City. Jennifer is a MFA candidate only because she likes bodies. And where on earth to find a better collection of bodies than upon a private liberal arts college in the United States? Already wealthy, Jennifer was going to be rich. Really rich. She tried not to think about this. Had Jennifer been Fern (before Jennifer agreed to become Fern), she

would have Googled her. Jennifer never played
the part of the pauper. But it was fun—
exciting, even—to let Jennifer assume, what
with her clothing and her position and her
condo, that she (the sort of woman who would
willingly abdicate her name!) was in control.
That she had the power.

Jennifer did not know why she created
what she created. There was a part of her—a
small feature of her that she did not
understand, and that which, she knew,
produced those paintings others found
valuable—that knew she was a fraud. An
impostor. This aspect of living was terrible.
She imagined that great artists operated from
something far greater than desire, or
inspiration. Jennifer simply wanted to paint
that which she found pretty. But pretty did not
sell. So, she pretended. She acted. When
painting to sell, Jennifer first fashioned
something amazing. And then, after a period
of time, she vandalized her work, installing,
visually, that which she knew the voyeurs and
the vultures would find irresistible. You might
not be able to account for taste, but, Jennifer
learned, taste was easy to manipulate. She had
vowed to never fully embrace fame.
Unfettered, she would, one day, produce.
Finding Jennifer (that woman who, like a
woman to a man, would give her name) made

this easier. But celebrity is difficult to deny.
For now, it was easy to have it both ways. She
refused to interview. When her agent insisted
that she comment, Jennifer said, "Call me
private. Better yet? Call me a pixel. Constantly
erased and reshaped. I don't retain. I create."

Did Fern (still Jennifer) intend more? Had
Jennifer (almost Fern) been looking to enter
into an argument? Probably not. She had long
suspected that Jennifer had a wide, far-
ranging capacity to drink—as in drinking
deliberately, just to get drunk—but this truth,
made visible, became no less disturbing
because of the veracity of her assumption.
Jennifer was not a mean drunk, but she was
not a sleepy, or docile drunk, either. Her ego
blossomed. Her rhetoric, while surprisingly
pretty, was loose. Wispy. Like the beta's tail
fanning the water. Her thoughts—which, when
sober, arose as quickly as they were varied—
accelerated in a direct correlation with her
ability to speak less proficiently. And so her
words, like mucus, dripped from her lips.
Strangely, Jennifer's logic became less
circular, and more sharply geometric, as if her
side of the conversation had assumed another
dimension. And Jennifer (still Jennifer) had
grown tired of it.

Jennifer had friends. Fern (still Jennifer)
did not, but she understood that part of being

in a relationship involved, at some point, going out. It was important for the women to learn aspects of one another other than the colors of their bras and the contours of their birth marks. They dressed up and went to installations, or to art houses, and from there to house parties, and from those to bars, Jennifer (not quite yet Fern) high on whatever, and Jennifer drinking whatever, whenever, and she was fun, and sexy, and charming, until she wasn't.

They were at Felicia's Atomic Lounge. It had been a quiet evening, quite fun, actually, one of those warm nights with nothing to do, and Jennifer (hours, now, from becoming Fern) had a martini, and was sipping a glass of merlot. She reached into her pocket and freed a few pills, swallowing a couple, and positioning a few between her gum line. One tasted bitter, and the other like mint. The world was warm. There was a glow. So far, the conversation had been wonderful. Drunk, and drinking, Jennifer had opened up, revealing facets of her past before this evening impossible to construct. To imagine.

By now the Jennifers had been together long enough to have been irritated, both one with the other, several times over. Only neither had given voice to register complaint, to openly find fault with the other. Looking back, Fern could not remember what, expressly, had prompted her to speak, to, for the first time, acknowledge—after finding, and considering—a criticism. She could not remember why she had been so bothered. She supposed her reaction had been natural. Drugs were fun. Drunks were a bore. At the time, though, she was surprised. There arose within her a sharp, pointed anxiety. The muscles in her back tensed. Jennifer understood, but could not believe, that she was nervous. She was conscious of her heart beating. That her eyes—lunar, crescent moons of thought—were not windows. She listened to herself speaking. Observed her finger pointing. She said, "That's quite a collection of straws you've got there."

Waiting, Jennifer considered Jennifer. The bar was dark. Her face moonlit. Blue. A shadow, absent feature, Jennifer recently had her hair done. The result? Less Uma Thurman and more Natalie Portman. Jennifer (it won't be long now) knew she would be unable to describe herself to a forensic artist. She did not have control over the diction needed to describe her nose. Her chin. She would use words like classical, probably. Not once did she ever think the composite resembled the criminal. It was only when the drawing was posted alongside the apprehended suspect's taken photograph that she could make out the similarities. And she was never blown away. The sketches were probably effective, but, ultimately, weren't they more a waste of time than beneficial? A means to satiate whomever? Before picking this fight, they had been talking about police sketches, yes? And Jennifer had still managed to softly insult her? Jennifer (still Jennifer) considered the efficacy of prayer. If it was prayer that created the God who had delivered unto her this Jennifer. If it was this self-same God who answered anyone's prayers. Jennifer (almost Fern!) watched Jennifer finish her Long Island Iced Tea. She watched Jennifer grab her purse, slide from her chair, stumble, straighten, pause, and, with a hand, toss back her head.

If this decision had been made so that the couple could argue in earnest, or without drawing unwanted attention, Fern—still Jennifer—would have been surprised. Jennifer, even when sober, was not the sort to care. Their leaving, though. This certainly played, for whatever the reason, no small part in what happened. The sudden introduction of fresh air functioned like an accelerant, and it was less than a block before the Jennifers hit their flashpoint. Jennifer (the one who remains Jennifer) bobbing and weaving and shouting and yelling, a stream of non-sequiturs which, once parsed, made a certain sort of sense. And Jennifer (when did she become Fern?) calm and in control, bold, happy that Jennifer was drunk and at such a decided disadvantage, both in terms of controlling her thoughts and emotions, not to mention her gross—forget fine—motor skills, was interested more than angry. She tried not to smile.

What Fern (no longer Jennifer) remembers, she will never forget. And this, even now—and perhaps more than anything—is just how heavy Jennifer becomes when drunk. Like wrestling a weighted sort of water, Fern (is this what life was going to be like as a Fern?) worked to control, to contain Jennifer as she spilled her way through the streets, up the steps, down the hallway, and into Jennifer's apartment. Like damming a fractured force of energy, parts of Jennifer flopping and lolling over Fern who, smaller, and much slighter, was forced to anticipate the unpredictable and do her best to support her. Fern went with the crash. She did not work against it.

This did force Fern, however, to consider Jennifer in a less flattering light. How it was that she could feel her girth. (She had never before even assumed that Jennifer *had* girth.) How her apartment—they never spent time there—was kind of coarse. It was that she could feel the common hopelessness of

Jennifer as human being, and how it was she reeked the spongy sickly-sweet stink of processed alcohol which arose as particularly gross. Fern had seen Jennifer drunk, hammered even, but she had never seen Jennifer lacking composure. Absent grace.

Fern had no idea what just happened. They had only been together for a couple of months, but it was this night that Fern gave herself, and completely, over to Jennifer. Worse, Jennifer was oblivious, immune to what she, Jennifer—now Fern (it was tough, early on, to draw the distinction)—was feeling, the idea that she had forfeited herself some time much longer ago.

She wriggled out of her jeans and kicked off her socks. But she did not fully undress. There was something like security, or comfort (at least this evening), in leaving on her bra, panties, and t-shirt, with Jennifer lying naked there beside her, vomit in her hair. But, Fern supposed, looking at the ceiling, her eyes adjusting to the darkness, you needed nights like these. At least occasionally. The sort which produced a personal sort of madness. The kind of craziness that invites the real you out into the open. Fern understood that she knew Jennifer well enough so as to be able to forgive her behavior, to disregard the drunk and cull from the evening a pleasant amount

of exposed, or revealed—Fern was not sure
there was a difference—innocence and youth
to better shape and inform her understanding
of the woman to whom, at some point during
their argument, she had given her name. Fern
cared about Jennifer enough so as to want to
cast all aspersions aside. Such was the nature
of love before time had its way with what
could—but can never be—such a lovely
sentiment.

Warm, Fern turned Jennifer's hand and set
it to rest, palm up, beside her. She placed her
own hand upon it, aligning wrist against wrist.
Fern could feel Jennifer's pulse. Her hand was
much smaller, her fingers more slender. This
was not to say that Jennifer had big hands.
Fern wanted to find beauty, not fault, as
Jennifer's great truth. And not because she
had to. Not because she wanted to, as means
to justify having made a terrible mistake. No.
It was easier than all that. And Fern closed her
eyes. When you love someone. And Fern
considered the contours of Jennifer's bed.
When you really, really, love someone. And she
registered the smell of Jennifer's laundry
detergent. Why, these are just those things
you sometimes do.

It was late. It was early in the morning.
Fern closed her eyes. Later on today she
would open them. The room—the world—

would seem too bright. Until then, Fern prepared for sleep. She pulled the comforter up to her neck. Breathing slowly, Fern crossed her hands and waited.

Most Wonderful Time of the Year

Katharine Bost

"How do you know she isn't a serial killer?" Shawn's tinny voice asks. He insists on using speaker mode for *all* conversations. At least he's home instead of the library this time.

"For the tenth time, she's in my art class." It's spoken through clenched teeth because Florida decided to be cold this week.

"It's the artists you have to watch out for, Bailey." When he's not studying sports film to help our university's athletes not suck, he's studying *Criminal Minds* and believes himself to be an *Unsub Expert.*

He's really just a nerd who couldn't find a murderer if they... murdered him.

"Really." It's to humor him because he loves talking about this. Also I want to look busy because our city is sketchy at night—lots of drunken frat bros and other hoodlums—and this section is no exception. In addition to the dark haze glowing about, it's drizzling.

The cold mist chills my skin and frizzes my hair—a terrible combination. I hope the sketchpad in my backpack doesn't get too wet. I burrow more into my coat and listen to him drone on about why Reagan is going to harvest my organs.

"It's because she'll want you to stay with her forever," he concludes. "Somewhat romantic, but mostly twisted. We can't understand the way they think, but isn't it interesting?"

Aside from my mom, my brother is the most melodramatic person I've ever met. He needs to stop watching documentaries and start socializing with actual people.

"Reagan is not going to harvest my organs," I say as I cross the street to her apartment complex. A modern building, with sharp angles and bright colors. I adjust my backpack strap so it doesn't cut into my shoulder.

"She might, and then Mom would be pissed," he says. "She's already pissed you're not home yet."

"I need to finish this project."

It wasn't my idea to wait until the last minute, but Reagan is hard to pin down. Er. Not like—*pin* down, but—never mind.

She's busy. And I know what you're thinking: why didn't I partner with someone not quite the social butterfly? The answer is that Reagan is without a doubt... the hottest person I have ever seen.

Yes. I am shallow. Not openly, but it's there.

She's also the most talented person in our art class, and I wanted to see what we could create together. At least that's what I'm telling myself.

"Right," Shawn says. "Mom wants you to call her before you leave tomorrow. And to let her know if you're bringing a plus-one to Thanksgiving."

"Are you her messenger?" I break my own cardinal rule and put him on speaker, and text Reagan and let her know I'm at the building's gate.

"I wouldn't have to be her messenger if you would call her," he says. "You know she means well."

"Yeah, okay." My pulse quickens when my phone notifies me that Reagan has seen my text. "She could be less passive-aggressive with her *meaning well*."

"That will never happen," Shawn says, ever the optimist. A piercing crackle comes through the line, and I'm grateful I have the phone on speaker or else my eardrum would have ruptured.

"What the hell was that?"

"Eating Doritos," he mumbles between munches. I'm thankful I'm not witness to the spewing crumbs.

"Gross."

"Oh, hey," he says, probably in what he hopes is a casual voice. "I'm bringing a plus-one."

My world stops, and not just because Reagan descends the outside stairwell. Shawn is bringing a date to Thanksgiving?

Shawn has a *date*?

"What?" I hiss, taking him off speaker. I have fifteen seconds until Reagan is at the gate, and I need to make the most of it. "What happened to Sibling Code? What happened to Single in Solidarity?"

"It's not a big deal." He crunches, and I wince because he's *right* in my ear. "She's really cool. You'll like her."

"How long have you been dating? What's her name? Does she have a pulse?"

"Of course, she has a pulse," Shawn says with a forced chuckle, as if he didn't try to get away with a pulse-less date last year.

"Doesn't she have a, I don't know, a family to spend it with?"

"They live across the country, so I invited her to spend it with us. Anyway, Mom's here. She—"

"Gotta go, Reagan's letting me in!" I end the call before he can respond.

She raises her eyebrows as she unlatches the hinge.

Reagan is a bit of hipster, a touch of Joan Jett, one hundred percent Cindy Crawford. Tattoos crawl up her arms. Her eyeliner flares out into wings, and her lips are highlighted red. Her dark hair is always pulled back into a ponytail, and she wears a different headband every day. Today's is black paisley.

"Everything good?" she asks as I enter the courtyard. Even her voice is sultry, a low rumble that makes me swallow.

"Yeah, just family drama," I say, waving my hand. She watches the movement with a calculated gaze, her gray eyes like molten lead. "And my brother thinks you're a serial killer."

Her lips turn down at the corners, like she's considering it. With a tilted nod, she indicates the stairwell.

She says, "Sounds like a messy job and I get second-hand guilt whenever my friends do something morally questionable, so I probably wouldn't be the best serial killer."

"Comforting?" I offer as I follow her up the stairs. I wish the stairwell were wide enough so I could walk beside her, because I *loathe* walking behind people on stairs. There's nowhere to look that isn't the other person's butt.

The smile she tosses over her shoulder is blinding. Red lipstick is her color. Classy and vintage.

By the time we make it to her floor, I'm winded and trying not to show it. We walk the hallway to her place, and it's only slightly horrifying that she left the door unlocked.

Either I need to watch fewer of Shawn's murder documentaries, or Reagan needs to watch more.

Her apartment is neat and organized. Nothing like mine. My roommate is a dungeon master (in all aspects of the name), and she leaves props and books everywhere. The kitchen, the living area, the bathrooms, *my* room.

There aren't any riding crops or board games in Regan's apartment. Abstract art populates the walls, and thick textbooks rest on her bar top, stacked perfectly. The turntable in the corner feels out of place. Fleetwood Mac is playing.

"Did you want anything to drink? I have Baileys." She smiles. It's award-winning. She could resolve extraterrestrial wars with that smile. "Such a pretty name."

"I'm fine with water," I say, willing my cheeks to stop flaming at her compliment.

When I sip from the glass she hands me, I make note of how it smells like her perfume. Reagan has a distinct scent. Coffee and cotton candy. The kind of aroma I'd like to turn into a candle and light while I draw.

"I've got my easel set up in my room, which," she frowns, "might be a little forward. Hang on. Let me grab that. Do you need one, too?"

"No, no, I'm fine to just draw on the coffee table," I say as I approach it. The strap of my backpack slides from my shoulder and I let the bag drop to the ground with a thud.

Reagan reappears with her easel and sets it up near the turntable. "Is Fleetwood okay? I can put something else on." She barely looks at me when she talks, but it feels like all her attention is on me.

"It's perfect." I flop down on her couch and unzip my pack. "Any thoughts on how you want to combine our styles?"

Her red lips push into a pout as she stares at her easel. "Well, I figured we should probably stick to one of our strengths. If we go with pencil, I won't need this."

"I can do whatever."

Our easy-goingness is a little awkward. I wish she'd tell me what she wants to do and order me around. It's much easier to work on group projects when the other person assumes the role as leader.

"Did you make all these?" I gesture about the wall. Once again, she follows the movement of my hand.

"Yeah," she says after a heartbeat. "Old pieces. I haven't done anything good enough to frame recently."

"Maybe we can frame our project when it's done."

She smiles and moves to sit beside me on the couch. It sinks beneath her weight, and then she's rifling through her portfolio.

"I was thinking," she says, "we could make trees out of hands."

It's kind of a weird idea, but I nod like I'm following.

"That's not what I meant," she says, laughing a bit. She pulls the bandana from her forehead and ties it around her bicep. "You draw trees, and I like drawing hands. What if we used the outline of hands for trees?"

"Like have the fingers bend where they form the branches?"

"Yeah, exactly."

The lighting is dim. I'd expect in a place like this for the light to be bright, but I like the ambiance it creates. This close, I can smell her coffee and cotton candy scent.

"Cool idea," I say. "I'm down for it."

When she leans forward to set her paper on the table, a lock of her dark hair swings free now that it isn't confined by the fabric. It looks soft, and I imagine reaching out and stroking it.

Instead, ever graced by the social gods, I ask, "What kind of shampoo do you use? And conditioner?"

Her eyebrows furrow. "Tresemme," she says, sounding confused. She twirls the end of her hair. "Why?"

There are several ways I can answer this, but I feel like all of them are weird. "Ooh la la." She stares. No laugh. "It's just... the commercials."

She smirks and goes back to her page. "Funny."

I have a noticeably *no page* on front of me, so I work overtime to produce it.

Except when I go to find a new page in my sketchbook, there's... nothing. I have no blank pages, and I can't believe I freaking forgot to grab a new one.

"Here," she says, and she gently rips a page at the perforation for me. "I have plenty. And I have extra shampoo and conditioner if you need any."

"I'm—not usually this awkward." I pause. "Well, sometimes. I don't know."

"Your hands are shaking," she says.

Sure enough, when I glance down to my pencil, it's trembling between my finger and thumb.

Her palm touches the back of my hand, steadying it. "Are you nervous?" she asks.

Part of me wonders if maybe I've entered an alternate universe, where that piercing crumple from Shawn's line wasn't him rummaging through a bag of Doritos, but rather someone ripping my reality in half.

"Sometimes," I say.

"I'd love to know," she says, releasing my hand, "why trees inspire you."

It doesn't sound like much, but to me, it might as well be a proclamation of love. Anyone showing interest in my art is an instant Love Point.

"Drawing them is relaxing. Each stroke takes focus, every detail must have purpose. It makes me feel like *I* have a purpose." I can count her thick eyelashes and see a small indent on the bottom of her lip. A scar. "Growth, life, all that jazz. They live much longer than people, assuming they're not cut down for warmth or paper. And they're peaceful. Have you ever just hung out with a tree? They don't judge."

The skin near Reagan's eyes crinkle as she smiles. "We all love a good judgment-free zone," she says. "My art's a little different, so I'm glad you wanted to work with me. Sorry for waiting so long to get started."

"No worries."

"The holidays are always a busy time at work," she says, but I didn't know she worked anywhere. Makes sense, I don't know much about her other than *oh my gosh she's so pretty and talented.*

"I get that," I say. "Other than my family and avoiding my roommate, I don't have much of a life. So I've got free time to work on this."

My attention finds one of the paintings above the couch. It looks multidimensional, painted so shapes appear 3-D. The colors are vibrant, and I could probably stare at this picture for hours, contemplating its meaning. The longer I look, the lonelier I feel.

I say, "I wanted to tell you, before I forgot. I think you're an amazing artist."

Her lips twitch. "Before you forgot?"

"You said you hadn't done anything recently that's worth framing," I say, motioning about the room. "But all of this is phenomenal. I don't know if anyone's told you that lately, so I wanted to."

Her cheeks flush, and when she shifts her body, it's closer to me. I can't tell if she moved this way on purpose, but my skin thrums from the buzz of being this close.

"That's nice of you to say," she says. "Do you display your art?"

"No," I admit. "I'm not big on sharing. I guess I don't want to give anyone the opportunity to tell me they think my work sucks."

She chews the inside of her cheek. "Maybe. Or maybe you're not giving anyone the chance to tell you they find beauty in it."

"That's another cool thing about trees. They just are. They are imposing, and beautiful, and they exude this natural confidence. I don't embody any of that, so I admire it. Does that make sense?" I ask.

When I turn to her, she's frowning.

"One of the reasons I wanted to work with you was because of your shading," she says, staring down at our blank papers. "I was hoping you could teach me."

"I'm not sure how good of a teacher I'd be, but I can try."

"I'm a quick study," she says, and is it just me, or was that a little flirtatious?

"Why do you draw hands now? Your abstract is incredible. I mean, so are your hands, don't get me wrong. But you have so many abstract pieces up, and no hands."

"Hands are personal." Her cool eyes assess me, that same calculation behind her stare. "You can tell a lot about a person by their hands."

I hold mine in front of my face. They look like hands.

"Here," she says, moving closer. She cradles one of my hands in hers. Her palm is warm. Closer, the smell of coffee and cotton candy is even more intoxicating. "Look." She drags an index finger down my middle finger.

"I put my hand on a hot stove as a kid. One of those coiled burners. Mom was draining the pasta she'd just boiled, and I thought the red glow of the coils was pretty."

"Yeah. A siren's call." She traces the scar. "Do you know how many people have this exact scar?"

I shake my head.

"Probably no one," she says, turning her attention to my fingerprint. "And this? Completely original. Every hand is different, and it tells a story."

"I never thought of it like that."

When she looks at me, the eye contact stirs something electric in my stomach. My mouth dries. Her gaze flickers to my lips.

"Trees are the same way," I say.

She hums, never looking away from my lips. "They are. That's why I wanted to work together."

She's put thought into this, and that just makes her even more appealing. Even if we're cutting it close to the deadline, it's not because she's slacking off.

"I think you're really pretty," I say, and that is totally not what I meant to say.

"Is that why you wanted to work with me?" she asks.

"One of the many reasons," I admit.

"I love honesty," she says, her face inching closer. "I can be honest, too. I like your style, I like your art, and I like your hands. I like the story they tell, and I really want to learn everything they say about you."

Her breath hitches right before our lips touch, and I'm the one to close the remaining distance.

Even if my mom throws backhanded grenades about how I've never been in a meaningful relationship, she's wrong. I've dated people, I've had flings, relationships, whatever. But no one has kissed me like Reagan does.

It's like art in a singular moment. Her soft, red lips against mine. Memorizing time or creating it.

"We have time," I say when I pull away. "The deadline's not until next week."

"And I really like the way you think."

It's the incessant buzzing of my phone that wakes me up. I roll over. The light sears my eyeballs, and I barely make out that my roommate texted me a few times last night, requesting I not come home because she needed the living room for a DnD Orgy. Ugh.

Mom's calling. Even though I'd rather die than answer her, I know she'll just keep calling.

"Hello." My voice is sandpaper on rock, and the rock is winning. My cheek finds solace in the soft, cool pillowcase beneath me. Reagan has a nice bed.

"Hi, sweetie," Mom says. She always sounds chipper, even when it's... crap, it's noon. Reagan has blackout curtains, so the room is dark, but the red numbers on her alarm clock reveal the time.

"What's up?"

"Just making sure you're on your way home," Mom says. "I haven't heard from you."

"Right, right," I say, trying to keep my voice low so I don't wake Reagan. "I haven't called because I'm not heading back yet. I will soon. Had to finish my art project."

Okay, so maybe I haven't even *started* my art project, but Mom doesn't need to know that.

"You'll get caught in traffic if you don't leave soon." There's a pause on her line, as if she's covering the mouthpiece and yelling at someone—probably Shawn. "We were hoping you would be in town so we could go to dinner as a family, but that's okay. There's always next year."

She says it like I won't be there for Thanksgiving lunch tomorrow.

"I'll be there as soon as possible." Behind me, Reagan nuzzles into my shoulder blade. Her arm is lazily wrapped around my waist, the bare skin hot against mine.

"Don't pick up any hitchhikers," Mom jokes. "Unless their last name is Rockefeller."

"Okay, got it, I'll be sure to ask their last name before I offer them a ride."

"That's my girl," Mom says. "Oh, have you heard about your brother's girlfriend? She is the cutest little thing. He showed me a message she sent the other day—she is to die for. I could eat her up."

"Thankfully there will be a lot of turkey and stuffing so you won't have to resort to cannibalism," I say dryly.

"Don't be like that," she says. "You could find someone like that, too, you know. Someone you don't mind bringing around."

Reagan's soft breath tickles my shoulder.

"I'll see," I say. "Anyway, I've gotta get ready. I'll see you in a few hours."

"Love you!"

"Love you, too. Bye."

I've lost any hope that I might not have woken Reagan. Sure enough, she shifts beneath the covers, drawing me closer. She adjusts the sheets so they conceal us more, like our own private fort.

"Was that your mom?" she sleepily asks.

"Yeah," I say. "She expected me to be on my way home already."

Reagan leans away and flips the light on her bedside table. My eyes take a moment to adjust, and I blink away spots. She props herself up on her elbow, tracing lines on my arm with her fingertips. Goosebumps trail my skin where her fingers have been.

"Did you want to be on your way home already?" It's the first time she's sounded uncertain. In every interaction we've had, she's been confident. Now, she seems more vulnerable.

"Definitely not," I say. "I'd miss Thanksgiving if it meant hanging out with you."

That makes her laugh. She pushes her hair out of her face and rolls her eyes. "Smooth talker," she says, kissing my shoulder. "How far away is it?"

"Depends on how fast you drive, but usually only like four hours," I say. "Do you go home for Thanksgiving?"

A shadow of something unknown passes over her face, and I immediately regret asking. She rolls away from me and gets out of bed, sliding articles of clothing onto her body.

"Do you want coffee?" she asks.

Reagan's coffee is, unsurprisingly, wonderful. She knows how to combine the perfect amount of cinnamon, vanilla syrup, and sugar to create caffeinated ecstasy.

"You could open a coffee shop and sell this," I tell her.

She rubs one of the tattoos on her arm. The entwined koi fish. "If art doesn't work out, I'll think about it."

My water glass from the night before is still on the counter, and I sip from it before returning to my coffee.

"It's nice that your mom cares where you are," she says.

"Yeah, she means well, but she can be a little much," I say. Which is way too much

information to spill this soon into a...
partnership. Reagan's just being polite. "You
probably don't want to know my life story, so
I'll spare you."

Her attention flickers to my hands. "If I
didn't care," she says, "I wouldn't ask."

I don't know how hands can tell a story,
but I think it's cool that she's so infatuated
with them. Maybe it's something to believe in,
like religion or astronomy or the Chicago
Bears.

As I sit at the bar, I sigh. "Mom's great, but
she's never accepting. I don't mean like she
thinks I should do something more sustainable
than art or she thinks I should be attracted to
guys. I don't entirely know how to word it, but
she never seems happy with what I'm doing. I
always could be doing something better."

"She pushes you," Reagan says, watching
me over the rim of her coffee mug.

"I don't mind that," I say quickly, because I
don't want her to think I'm lazy. "I just want
her to be more direct about it."

"Ah." She sets her mug down. "Passive
aggressive."

"Exactly."

"Bummer." She drums her fingers on the
surface of the counter.

"And," I say, "Thanksgiving is going to be
worse because my brother is bringing a date."

Reagan doesn't seem to see why this is catastrophic.

"Now Mom is going to focus only on me, since I'm the one who doesn't have someone to share the holidays with. Since I don't have someone to share with the *family* during the holidays," I say.

"It must be nice to have a family that close," she says, and I get the weirdest idea I've ever had.

But it might not be *that* weird. I mean, we just "hung out" all night and morning. We're acquaintances. We've been in the same art classes the last three semesters.

"You look very much in thought," she says.

"This is weird, but I'm going to throw it out there. If you don't have Thanksgiving plans, do you want to be my date to my family's celebration?" I ask. "Obviously, all fake. We don't really know each other. We've had *classes* together, and we got to know each other a lot last night, but we still don't completely *know* each other. But it'd keep my mom from hyperfocusing on me. You'd get delicious food. I'd pay you if you wanted. I've heard of these, like, HoliDate Services where you can pay a person to be your date. It could be like that, only no third party."

Reagan's smile fades. She looks at the clock over the sink. "I wish I could," she says, and it sounds like she means it, which is... a shock. "I have this other thing."

It stings, but I get it. She has a life. She has her own family.

"We'll have to get together when you get back, though," she says. "And not just because we have to finish the art project."

That sounds... nice. Her smile is soft, and I find myself nodding.

"For the record," she says later as I'm leaving, "you wouldn't have to pay me to be your date."

Once I arrive home, I'm bombarded by family wondering where I've been. It took me a little longer than normal because of traffic (Mom was right), but they all act like they would never see me again.

Thankfully, Aunt Ida takes this time to recapture the audience's attention when she lets everyone know about the new smashed potatoes recipe she's trying tomorrow.

As soon as everyone is tired of bugging me about getting in late, and tired of hearing about Aunt Ida's recipe, the conversation turns to Shawn's girlfriend. It quickly becomes the only thing anyone talks about until Thanksgiving.

We celebrate with a lunch because people drive in from other areas, and they don't want to get a late start driving home. Thanksgiving is a spectacle in my family—everyone brings like two dishes apiece, and so we always have way too much food and no space to put it. Last year, we had to put the chip dip bar on the grand piano.

My parents' house is quickly filled with aunts, uncles, cousins, and cousins' kids who no one can remember the names of. I try to stay under the radar.

"Bailey, will you help me with this?" Mom asks as she hoists a pan of green bean casserole onto the stove. "Just close the oven— yes, good, that burner is hot, so don't touch it."

It's something Mom reminds me all the time, even though I was literally two when I did that. But it also reminds me of Reagan, and her tracing the scars left behind.

Mom suddenly stops bustling about the kitchen. She straightens, wiping her hands on her apron. "Oh my goodness," she says.

"What?" Alarmed, I look around the kitchen—did she forget silverware again? Napkins? Do I need to run to the store?

"She's here." Mom sucks in a deep breath. "She's *here*."

"Who's here?"

"Jennifer," Mom says. "I felt her car pull into the drive."

Right. Jennifer. Shawn's girlfriend. The one no one can stop talking about.

"What do you mean you *felt* her car—?"

Mom shoves past, almost knocking me into the cranberry sauce. As she parades toward the front door, she lets *everyone* know who has just arrived. Shawn is nowhere to be seen—probably outside warning Jennifer about our insane family.

Sure enough, the family flocks to the front door like a pack of wolves waiting for a broken lamb to stumble into their line of sight.

It's my duty as a sister to support Shawn, so I push my way through the throng of people, only getting elbowed by Uncle Terry once. Shawn is going to owe me big time. First, he brings a date—I didn't even know he *had* a girlfriend—and now I'm going to throw them a lifeline whenever the waters are too rough.

Shawn walks inside, Jennifer behind him. He's skinnier than a telephone pole, so his shoulders only partway cover her, but I can't see what she looks like. Judging by her green dress, she's stylish. So that's a win for Shawn.

Then he moves, and everything stops.

That's not Jennifer.

That's Reagan.

This isn't exactly how I imagined Thanksgiving going.

Oh my gosh.

When Reagan said she had other plans, she didn't say she had another *life*. Oh my God, I hooked up with my brother's girlfriend!

There is no way to hide the panic from my face. Reagan doesn't look any better. When our gazes meet, her winning smile drops. Her eyes widen, and she looks at Shawn in her peripheries.

We're having a joint Oh, Shit Moment.

Shawn is clueless as he hangs their jackets up on the coatrack. "Everyone, this is Jennifer." To Reagan, he says, "Don't worry about getting everyone's names. There are a lot."

Reagan looks out of her element. Her normally collected face is red, and her eyes keep darting back to me. Occasionally, she gives me a once-over. I'm not sure if she's judging my outfit choice or what, but I didn't get the memo that we were supposed to dress adorably. I'm wearing an ugly green reindeer sweater and black leggings, which is nothing compared to her festive holiday dress.

She looks *adorable*, but there's no headband in sight. Instead, a red bow ties half of her hair back. Even her makeup is different. No winged eyeliner or red lipstick.

Shawn fires off everyone's names, and Reagan nods like she knows what the hell he just said. But to my surprise, she's able to repeat them without any hesitation. Her voice noticeably shakes when she says my name.

God exists, because Aunt Ida asks if anyone wants to look at the mole on her big toe, and everyone flees, suddenly very interested in any room that does not house Aunt Ida.

Once it's just Mom and me remaining, Shawn wraps his arm around Reagan. She leans into him and flashes Mom a grin that doesn't make my stomach flip.

"Do you know each other?" Shawn asks, because I think I still look shocked.

"We were in the same art class last semester," Reagan says. Her cheeks are tight.

Yes. We were. And that's not where she modeled nude for me.

"Yeah," I say. "She drew... hands."

Reagan offers a polite laugh, which is better than Mom and Shawn's matching blank expressions.

"Honey, sweetie," Mom says to them, "come sample some of the cheese. We have brie this year, and it's delectable."

"I *love* brie," Reagan says in an overly happy voice I don't recognize. She brushes past me without another word, and I try to wrap my mind around what is happening.

I think I slept with my brother's girlfriend. Oh my God, I'm such a horrible person. But she's worse! She knew she was dating someone! I had no idea. No, it doesn't matter. I should have seen this coming. I'm a homewrecker.

And Shawn... how did this happen? I mean, I'm a dork, sure, but Shawn is the Epitome of Dork. He's such a dork that my roommate didn't want him to join her DnD group. That's right. He was rejected by the rejects.

"So, Jennifer," I say slowly, but the name is weird in my mouth. That's not Jennifer. Is it? Has this entire thing been a con? Is Reagan a fake name?

"Yeah," he says. "She's something, right?"

"Yeah," I say. "Um, how did you...?"

"Through a mutual friend," he says. It sounds like he's reading from a script. "We hit it off immediately."

"You and... Jennifer."

He nods, a little too quickly. "Yeah, me and Jennifer. Not me and the friend. We were already friends."

"What do you and Jennifer talk about?"

"Talk?" He clears his throat and shrugs. It's a pathetic half-shrug, like he changed his mind midway through the motion but his shoulders didn't get the memo. "All kinds of things. She loves *Criminal Minds* and documentaries, too. We can talk for hours about that."

"You met a girl who talks about your fan theory that Prentiss and JJ are actually in love?"

He scratches his arm and shifts his weight to his heels. "She agrees."

Of *course* she agrees. Every sapphic who watches that show agrees. How does that not fire warning bells in his head?

"What do you think of her art?" I ask. "Her paintings?"

"Breathtaking." His eyes dart around the room, stopping at the dining area, where we see Aunt Ida has cornered Reagan into listening to a story about her teacup poodles.

"A foul stench permeated the house for many months until I realized that they were sneaking beneath the couch to pee every time I turned my back," Aunt Ida says.

Shawn grimaces. "Gotta go," he says, punching my arm. "I don't want to leave her alone for too long. The family might freak her out."

Valid concern. I wave him off, still reeling.
Then one of my cousins (James? Jeffrey?) kicks
the back of my knee and my legs give out, and
I end up prone on the ornate rug of our
entryway.

It seems entirely applicable.

Lunch goes about as well as I had
expected. The same cousin who deadlegged
me in the previous section had an allergic
reaction to Aunt Ida's smashed potatoes. He's
apparently allergic to potatoes, which, in a
twist of fate that surprised absolutely no one,
triggered his reaction.

In addition to this tragedy (he's fine now,
but would probably be better if we could
remember his name), Mom constantly fawned
over "Jennifer." I've known Reagan for over a
year, and I don't think I've ever seen her smile
this much. It looks nice on her, but it's also
unfamiliar.

Everyone loves learning about Jennifer,
since she's the fresh blood. Other than an
occasional glance in my direction, the
spotlight doesn't bother her. She soaks up the
attention like my sweater soaked the gravy I
dropped on it earlier.

The plot thickens during dessert. Mom has
dished The Golden Couple two pieces of pie,

and they're sharing a fork. Shawn lets Reagan do most of the talking, and she's good at it. Too good.

"Shawn tells me you're an accounting major," Mom says and that raises Major Red Flags.

I may not know Reagan *that* well, but she's definitely an art history major. She told me the other night, while we were avoiding our project. I don't know what it is about this whole situation, but I want it to be a lie. I want to catch Reagan in this lie. She's pretending to be someone else, but why? Does Shawn know who she really is?

I try to ignore the thought cropping in my head that I want it to be a lie because I don't want to be the bad person here. The homewrecker.

"Yeah," Reagan says, and this time, the look she spares me is longer than a glance. "I used to be an art history major, thus the class with Bailey, but my parents thought accounting would be more suitable in the long run."

"Very smart," Mom says. "Bailey." She looks at me and tilts her head down, implying *Are you taking notes*?

I ignore her and shovel more pie in my mouth. After I swallow, I ask, "How long have you been together?"

Now it's Shawn who's giving me a dirty look. "A few months." He wraps his arm protectively around Reagan. I don't like how his fingers brush her skin because it reminds me of what I did with her the other night.

What the hell is she playing at?

Mom taps Reagan's wrist. "I haven't shown you the Christmas album yet. Do you want to see?"

"Absolutely," Reagan says with an easy smile. She doesn't look at me again, even though I know she can feel me glaring at her.

As soon as we're alone, I round on Shawn. He's very invested in his pie. "Why didn't you tell me you were dating anyone?"

He shrugs. Must be difficult to respond when he's stuffing his face. "Never came up."

Never came up? He lives right down the hall. We get dinner every weekend. It doesn't make sense that he wouldn't say anything.

"How long have you been dating Reagan?"

"She doesn't go by Reagan," Shawn says. He has the audacity to roll his eyes. "Everyone who knows her uses her middle name."

That... can't be true. I know Reagan. I know her a hell of a lot better than Shawn does.

"Earlier, you said her paintings were breathtaking." It's impossible to let this go. Whoever he's talking about isn't the same girl

I stayed up with in the late hours the other night. She isn't the same one who had such great ideas about hands and trees. "What's breathtaking about them?"

"They're art," he says. "Just like how your drawings are amazing. Beauty is in the eye of the beholder."

"Yeah, but what *makes* them amazing?"

"She makes them amazing." He pushes pie about his plate before scooping a hunk onto his fork. "She's the most talented person I know, and I'm really lucky."

"She's not who you think she is," I say. This entire situation that has me so *hot* and annoyed and I'm just sick of my family. Sick of my mom treating me like I'm a child who's going to burn their hand again, sick of my brother lying to me about dating someone, sick of the girl who I thought liked me that is apparently dating said brother. Everything is annoying and I want to scream.

"She's exactly who I think she is."

"You're being stupid," I say. "You have no idea. Reagan—that's her name—she's the girl I'm working on the art project with."

Shawn's eye twitches, and he stuffs the heaping pile of pie into his mouth. "Her name's Jennifer." Bits of pecans ricochet from his mouth. "She doesn't go by Reagan, and you're being weird."

"I'm not being *weird*, I'm telling you that she—that I—that we—"

"Look, just because you're sad about your own life doesn't mean you can tease me about mine. Jennifer really likes me, and I know that may be weird for you, but she's the first girl who sees me for who I am. Who likes the dorky sides that other girls scoff at."

A small, sisterly part of me understands this. He seems so defeated, and I want to reach out and give him a hug.

But a bigger, jealous part of me rears its head. It overshadows any sympathy I would want to show. It bubbles beneath my skin, and my fingers tremble.

"You're insane," I say, my voice shaking. It feels good to put this in the open. "Your girlfriend's name is Reagan, and I slept with her the other night. Did she tell you about that? Since you guys have such great conversations about *Criminal Minds*, maybe she let it slip that we slipped in her bed. Naked."

Shawn's temple tics as I speak, but by the time I've uttered the word *naked*, he snaps. He stands up, his chair shooting out from behind him, and he throws his fork on the table. It clatters and falls to the floor.

If people weren't listening to us before, they're listening now.

"You're such a *baby*, Bailey," he says. "Everything has to be about you. God, I can't believe you're this upset over my dating life. Are you so starved for attention that you have to make up stories about my girlfriend? Jennifer isn't interested in you."

The raised voices bring Mom and Reagan back into the kitchen doorway. A photo album is pinned between Mom's arm and her side, and Reagan has a fistful of pictures in her hand. Her mouth is open, and she's dividing her attention between Shawn and me.

"Her name isn't *Jennifer*, oh my God," I say, throwing my hands up. "It's *Reagan*. And whatever the hell this game is, it isn't funny."

"Ask her!" Shawn yells. "Ask her what her name is!"

Reagan looks like the possum you'd see when you open your garbage lid in the early morning. Wide eyes, wide mouth, searching the corners for an exit strategy.

"What's your real name, Reagan? Is it Jennifer?"

"Don't talk to her like that!"

"You told me to ask her what her name is!"

The room goes quiet, save for Shawn and my heavy breathing. "Um," Reagan says, but it does little to fill the hungry void.

"Kids, remember the importance of family!" Mom says.

"It's a simple question, Reagan," I say, and I know I shouldn't direct my anger at *her*, but I'm still pretty pissed off with her. On one hand, if she *is* Shawn's girlfriend, she had sex with me while dating him. If she's not, then why didn't she tell me anything? Why did she lie?

My tone of voice must annoy Shawn, because he starts to reprimand me. "Bailey, you—"

Mom cuts in. "You two are *adults*, and you should start acting like it. What will the children think? What will Aunt *Ida* think?"

"Oh," Aunt Ida says, happy to be addressed. "I think they are acting like my teacup poodles. Neither of you can fit underneath the couch, can you?"

I'm seething. "I don't give a damn what anyone else thinks. Shawn is either lying about dating Reagan, or Reagan lied to me. Either one pisses me off. What's the truth, Reagan? Is your name Jennifer? Did you cheat on my brother? Or are you pulling wool over our eyes?"

The photos in Reagan's hands crumple. She seems to notice their bent corners, and she comes back to herself, using her leg to straighten the photos again. "I'm sorry," she says to my mom. "I ruined the pictures." Her

voice is small. Tears shimmer in her eyes. "I'm
so sorry, I ruined Thanksgiving for everyone."

"Jennifer," Shawn says, reaching out for
her. "Baby, you don't have to go."
"It's Reagan," she says with her back to him.
"You know my name is Reagan."

And then she leaves, all of us watching her
retreat with our mouths agape. I look at the
surroundings—there is food everywhere (when
did we become such a messy family?), random
family members are strewn about, and Mom is
crying.

"Did she say she ruined Thanksgiving?"
Aunt Ida asks. "This is the best one yet."

"Blood is thicker than water," Mom says,
ignoring Ida. "You two should be able to
discuss these things like adults."

Shawn says nothing. He stares at the front
door and gnashes his teeth.

"She said you knew what her name was," I
say, but my tone is much gentler than it was
earlier. "What did she mean?"

He stoops over to pick the fork up off the
ground. Bits of pie litter the rug beneath the
table, but Shawn ignores it. "It's Reagan," he
whispers. "I hired her." He drops into one of
the chairs and covers his face.

"Hired her?" It's Mom who asks. "Why on
earth would you hire her?"

"Where on earth?" Aunt Ida adds.

"From the HoliDate website," Shawn says. His voice is muffled by his hands. "I'm sorry. I wanted to not be a loser for once. I thought if I brought a date, everyone would stop calling me a virgin."

"Honey, who calls you that?"

Shawn's shoulders lift to his ears. "You and Bailey tell me if I don't stop watching documentaries, I'm never going to find someone to bring home."

"That's not—we don't actually mean it," Mom says. That doesn't sound like her. "Or at least I don't."

That sounds more like her.

"I'm just giving you a hard time," I say, feeling scolded. "I didn't know it bothered you."

"It does!" Shawn says. "It's embarrassing. Kind of like, well, this interaction right now, in front of the whole family."

"Uncle Leo died almost six years ago exactly," Aunt Ida says. "So it isn't the whole family."

This is holiday drama I never knew could exist. I never knew my teasing bothered Shawn, but standing here, I realize I said some pretty mean things to Reagan.

The front door opens, and Reagan slides into view. "Um, can whoever owns the silver Taurus move their car? I'm blocked in."

Aunt Ida springs to life. "That's my cue! Let me go piddle first."

Reagan smiles, but it looks forced. "Thanks, Aunt—thanks, Ida."

I watch her walk out the front door again, and it's even worse than the first time. But she can't leave until Aunt Ida moves her car, so I know I have time.

Even with my mom and Shawn still having a heart-to-heart, I head toward the door. I ignore their commands for me to come back.

Reagan is waiting in her car when I hurtle out of the house. I slip on a puddle of water and all but slam into the side of her car. The locks click, and at first I think she's locking me out, but she's unlocked them.

I slip into her car, happy to be enveloped by the warmth.

"Hi," I say. The atmosphere is charged with tension, and my teeth chatter.

"Hi."

"I owe you an apology for being a jerk," I say. "I was just so confused on what was happening. Before I knew it, I was going all *Jersey Shore* on you."

"I didn't realize people still watched that show," Reagan says, but her voice is distant and she's looking out the front window. Anywhere but me, really.

"They don't," I assent. "I'm sorry I was a jerk. I'm embarrassed by how I acted."

Reagan continues to stare. Her fingers wrap around the steering wheel. "I'm the one who should be embarrassed."

I start to say "There's no need," but I also want to hear what she thinks, so I awkwardly motion for her to continue.

"I started the HoliDate services a few years ago, when my parents died."

Whatever I had been expecting wasn't that. I watch her knuckles tighten, and if I were braver, I'd hold them.

"My grandparents died when I was young, and my parents were both only children," she says. "I have no one to spend the holidays with."

Her hands slide from the steering wheel and she sits on them. "I thought the services was the perfect solution. I didn't like being alone, I would get paid, and I'd save people from embarrassing 'You're still single' family conversations. It felt like a win in every direction."

This time, I am brave enough to place my hand on her leg. Goosebumps prickle her skin.

"But it's not," Reagan says. "I used to paint a picture after every holiday to track my emotions. It was always lonely. Even though I'd be surrounded by all these people, I still felt alone. No one actually wanted me there." She swallows. "It's clear that the pathetic one in all of this isn't Shawn. It's me."

"You're not pathetic," I say. "Nothing you say makes me think that. I just wish—I wish you had told me."

"He'd already paid me," Reagan says. "When I saw it was you, I panicked. I didn't know if Shawn wanted me to say anything, so I kept quiet."

"He told everyone just now," I say as Aunt Ida flops into her car. She waves out the window to us, as if we don't know she's in there.

Slowly, her car putters forward. It's like watching Austin Powers trying to get his service vehicle unstuck from the hallway.

"We should go somewhere." I squeeze her leg, and she finally looks at me.

"Yeah?"

"I don't want this Thanksgiving to give you another negative inspiration for your abstract art," I say. "Actually, I want you to be content enough to draw hands. My hands, maybe?"

"Maybe," Reagan says with an arched brow.

"Let's go, then," I say. "Let's salvage Thanksgiving."

"Won't your family be mad?"

"It might be time to care less about what people think," I say. "Be more like a tree."

"I think," Reagan says as she starts the car, "that might have been more poetic in your head."

And So She Returned

Ashe Thurman

It was another hot summer. Every year they said this summer was hotter than the one before, but if that was the case, they'd have all melted into the concrete years ago. Charlotte rocked back and forth on the glider on the front porch of her parents' house. Her dad brought her out a glass of iced tea, setting it on the side table (being sure to use a coaster) then scurrying back inside. He was still weird around her since…well… It had gotten better, though. His discomfort would fade over time. Her mother, for her part, had put a little striped "ALLY" sticker on the back of her fancy white hatchback, just below the large sticker cutout advertising her Etsy shop selling quirky vinyl cut paraphernalia for the #momlife set. She wasn't totally convinced her mom actually understood the full weight of the idea, yet, though, either.

She gazed down the old road, the air wavering with heat. The sound of a car coming up over the hill made her tense with anticipation. It was Mrs. Grady from down the street, her twenty-year old minivan coughing and sputtering on the steep incline. The next one was a huge, spic and span dualie with a trailer hitch that had probably never been used. She didn't recognize it, but it was probably one of the teenage boys up at the top of the hill. The Dunlap clan had about six of them if she remembered right. The third oldest was the same age as her, and they had had something resembling a friendship for most of high school. He was living somewhere out on the west coast working a job with an unnecessarily long title in a field she had only an abstract understanding of. She hadn't seen him in person since they shared a class for a semester at the most local branch of the community college, getting their gen-eds out of the way. He had gone across the country to finish out school. She had stayed closer, commuting into the city for a few semesters until she got her certifications. She wasn't surprised their only communication had turned into sharing vague reactions on Facebook posts. He had escaped.

The next car was coming up the road. It was quiet. It glinted in the sun. It was a newer car, a four door compact sedan in beige. It slowed as it approached the house.

It was her. Her profile was unmistakable: an abundance of black, curly hair that she just managed to make behave with a card of bobby pins and a prayer. As the car slowed, the woman inside it started waving excitedly. The window rolled down.

"Chaaaaarrrlloooootttteeee!" she called.

Charlotte was running down the front porch steps before her brain could catch up to her feet. She threaded her arms through the car window and around the woman's shoulders. They squeezed each other.

"It took you long enough to get here," Charlotte said as she pulled away.

"The rental place at the airport didn't know what they were doing, and I had to get a manager involved. It was ridiculous. But, oh my god look at you! I almost didn't recognize you! You look good as a brunette." Charlotte rubbed the back of her head where, until a few years ago, cascades of stick straight blond hair had hung limply down past her shoulder blades.

"You know I always threatened to cut it short. Finally just went ahead and did it." Charlotte smiled, tucking a piece of stray fringe behind her ear.

The woman patted the passenger side seat.

"Hop in! We've got soooo much catching up to do."

Charlotte shook her head.

"Go ahead and go on up to the house. My purse and stuff is inside, and I'm not even wearing my shoes." She wiggled her toes again the hot sidewalk. She hadn't thought about it before running down to meet the car. "I'll meet you up there, okay?" The woman shrugged, waved, and zoomed up off the road. Charlotte walked back up to the front door of the house. Her purse was sitting on the entryway table. She grabbed it and slipped on her sandals. She scuttled back through the door, calling to her parents that she was off, and paused at the top step of the porch. She sighed and started walking.

Alyssa was back.

For the first eleven years of Charlotte's life, Alyssa was the girl down at the corner who went to the Catholic school. Alyssa didn't have a daddy but that wasn't the kind of thing you talked about. They were the only two girls of the right age on the block, so they played together sometimes on Saturday afternoons.

On the first day of sixth grade, Charlotte walked into the middle school with hands shoved in her pockets, nervous. Until an arm came through hers and started dragging her up the path. Alyssa had convinced her mom to let her go to the public school.

They became inseparable, then. Their personalities clicked and locked in, and they grew into their impending womanhood as a pair. Not without a misstep (or two or three or four), but that was life and they were happy to be living it together.

It was the first cold day of their sophomore year of high school when things began to change.

Already well into November (because that's when winter truly started to take hold), they huddled together under a blanket in Alyssa's living room, watching a movie that wasn't as scary as they thought it would be, shooting popcorn into each other's mouths.

"You know that guy I met this summer," Alyssa had begun teasingly when they had gotten more food on the ground than in their stomachs.

Charlotte looked at her sideways. Alyssa and her mother had spent a week visiting family over summer vacation. There had been a beach involved and a boy. That part had struck a chord with Charlotte for some reason. Of course, neither of them had had any grand romantic overtures, yet, but Alyssa had become especially prone to wandering her eyes over every masculine form that passed their way. Examining them, appraising them. It was all talk and conjecture, still, but it made Charlotte feel uneasy. Charlotte didn't really see boys the way Alyssa did, though, so she wrote her discomfort off as jealousy or a lack of understanding. They had always been in step. It was only a matter of time before they synced up again.

"Well..." and Alyssa rolled her eyes dramatically. "You know, we were down at the beach, at it was dark, and there was no one around, so we...kinda..." and she raised her eyebrows suggestively.

Charlotte took a moment to understand. "You did...*it.* Like...IT?"

Alyssa hushed her quickly, but her mom wasn't even home to overhear them. There wasn't anybody around who would care. Charlotte pushed Alyssa in the shoulder. Alyssa rolled away, then back.

"Are you serious? We agreed that we were gonna, like, wait until we had boyfriends and we were ready and stuff." Something dark welled up from the bottom of Charlotte's stomach.

"Are you mad?" Alyssa seemed gcnuinely contrite.

"No, I'm not mad...just...why? I mean...some guy you don't know?"

Alyssa shrugged.

"I don't know. I was just curious, I guess. I just wanted to know what it was like, and I figured why wait? I mean, it's not like it's that big a deal."

"I mean, I guess...I don't know. Why are you telling me now, though? Why didn't you tell me then?"

Alyssa looked at the floor.

"I don't know. I guess it just didn't seem...fair to you? Like, I was still a little weird about it, and I didn't want to make you mad. I don't know. Whatever. I mean, I told you now, so that's okay, right?" Her words sort of swam together, hesitant, uncertain.

"No, it's fine. Just...tell me more about it later." Alyssa smiled at her, but she knew that it wasn't reaching all the way up her face. She started picking at the carpet with her fingers. That dark feeling was in her chest, now, and was threatening to overtake her. Why, though? Was it jealousy? Was it annoyance that Alyssa had been so brash? But then it wasn't even any of her business what Alyssa did with her own body. What could this sensation be?

Alyssa decided, on what seemed like a whim, that she wasn't going to take that scholarship to the state university. She was going to go to Europe and backpack across it. To most it seemed like just the frivolous kind of thing that Alyssa would do, but Charlotte knew. She knew about the pregnancy scare their junior year after the boy Alyssa was dating wasn't too keen on taking no for an answer. She knew how her mom's decision to start dating again had made Alyssa feel like she wasn't as important. None of the boyfriends her mom had brought home had ever been anything but kind to her, but Alyssa and her mom had spent the last three years fighting it out. Charlotte knew about the cigarettes and the pot and the drinking and the anti-depressants. Charlotte had been there when Alyssa found out who her biological father was and suffered with her through the realization she would have been better off not knowing. Alyssa was scared of what she was and scared of what she was becoming. She needed to get away, and Charlotte saw it coming before even Alyssa did.

A few weeks after graduation, Charlotte was the one to borrow her dad's pickup truck to take Alyssa to the nearest airport an hour away. Together, they lugged the suitcase out of the bed of the truck onto the curb of the drop off lane.

"Well, this is it," Alyssa said.

Charlotte didn't reply. She just reached out and hugged her with everything she had. She had been prepping for this moment for months, and now she wanted it to end it as swiftly as possible. This was the moment when she would be letting Alyssa go. She had figured out, a long time ago, that this moment would have to come, that their friendship lived on borrowed time. Because over the past few years, the darkness she had first felt on that frosty winter night consumed her, and she came to know what those blighted and heavy feelings were.

Charlotte had fallen in love.

Charlotte knocked on the door, huffing a little. The walk down to Alyssa's old house had gotten longer somehow. She wiped the sweat from her forehead. The door made the sucking sound of new weather stripping as it opened. Alyssa's mom stood on the other side with a tray of vegetable skewers for the the grill. Enough food for three. She had anticipated this alright. Charlotte was ushered through the house and into the back yard to see that Alyssa had already been put on grill duty. She waved a spatula at Charlotte and beckoned her over. Charlotte took the space that belonged to her right at the front of the grill. They had done this so many Saturdays so long ago. Alyssa slid a popped beer into her hand.

That was pretty close to how things had been then, too.

"Man, how long has it been?" Alyssa cooed.

"Eight years," Charlotte answered immediately. Alyssa thought for a moment.

"Yeah, I guess that's right, isn't it. Damn. So, what all do we need to catch up on? You married, yet?" She was only joking, but there was a little pang of hurt. While the idea of finding anyone to settle down with long-term seemed distant and gray, the idea that she wouldn't invite Alyssa were a wedding to occur was almost insulting. Despite everything, Charlotte still cared for her deeply.

"No. Not really something that I think is gonna happen for me any time, soon. I know you're not, so I won't even bother asking."

"Oh? You just know these things about me."

"Your mom forwards me the e-mails you send her. I skim them."

"Stalker."

"Well, you don't e-mail me." There was silence. Even though Charlotte was the one who had wanted to push her away, it was Alyssa who had cut off all contact. For a year, it made sense; she was in some foreign country trying to make it work on her own. The first time anyone heard a peep from her was when she came back stateside and enrolled in a Southern Ivy League school.

Alyssa flipped the burgers.

"I thought you'd be better off without me for a while. I was so...destructive toward the end there. And I was so worried I'd bring you down with me, for a minute."

"But now it's okay to come back and hang out?"

"Well, my grandad kinda died so..." And Alyssa laughed. It was sad, of course, but she hated the guy. Her mom hated the guy. He wasn't a good man, and this knowledge wasn't limited to his immediate family. The funeral tomorrow would be filled with people lining the halls of his one-way trip to hell.

"And, well, I haven't told Mom, this, yet, but..." And she looked around to make sure her mom had gone back inside. "I got a really good job offer in the city, and I'm thinking about taking it. A few years ago, I would have been like 'hell naw,' but I'm all that Mom has left, you know? Maybe it's okay to stick around."

Charlotte was only half listening at this point, though. Alyssa moving back nearby? A ninety-minute drive on the new highway? Could she handle it? As she stood here next to her, now, she could feel those old creeping emotions sneaking in, but they were dulled

with age. Perhaps both their plans had
worked, and the separation had been the best
for them, in the end.

"Charlotte, honey." Alyssa's mom came
trotting out with more vegetable skewers.
"You were able to get off tomorrow to help me
with things in the morning, right?"

"I've got to go in really early and fix a
stocking error, but yeah, I'll be there for sure."

Alyssa turned to her slightly.

"Stocking? I thought you were working for
Dr. Kincaide?"

"No, I'm the assistant operations manager
at the grocery store, now."

"Oh? What happened?"

Charlotte felt herself squirming. She didn't
want to talk about this, right now, but it would
come up eventually.

"They just didn't need me anymore, and
there's only so many spots for a hygienist in a
town with only three dentists. But it's okay. I
actually really like it. I'm good at it, and I
pretty much run the place."

Alyssa nodded a few times that she
understood.

"Wait, hold, on," Charlotte had realized
something. "How did you know I was working
for Dr. Kincaid?"

Alyssa averted her eyes as she flipped the
burgers again.

"I, uh, asked Mom to keep me updated on what was going on with you."

Charlotte looked down and watched Alyssa's hands work the spatula. She felt herself smiling.

"Okay, so, these are from the Hague." Alyssa had a whole separate hard drive full of her Europe pictures, and they flipped through them idly. It was just like the evenings back in the old days, only they had replaced popcorn and illicitly acquired wine coolers with a cheese plate and boxed chardonnay.

"It's so pretty," Charlotte gushed.

"I'm thinking about going back this Christmas. You should come with."

"I don't know. I'd have to take off work, and I don't know if I could afford it."

"Oh, come on, where's your sense of adventure?"

"You've had enough adventure for both of us, I think. I didn't know about your stint volunteering with Doctors Without Borders."

"I was just doing fetch and carry stuff, but it's what got me my second scholarship so....meh."

"Was wondering how you managed to afford that fancy school of yours."

They kept flipping through pictures of buildings and statues. They paused on one of Alyssa and a pretty blonde in front of a fountain.

"Oh, she's pretty. One of your hostel buddies?"

Alyssa hesitated to answer, twitching her fingers on the keyboard.

"Yes? Actually, if you wanna know the whole truth we kinda...dated...for a little bit."

It was like every nerve in Charlotte's body was made of fire and ice all at the same time.

"You're into girls, now?"

Alyssa shimmied her shoulders in hesitance.

"Yeah. I mean...Joline was the first one and it was just supposed to be an experiment. But, yeah, I mean I've tried dating a couple of other girls since then, and I was really attracted to them and stuff, but girls are harder, somehow. I don't know. Maybe I'm better off sticking with men." Alyssa scratched her head. "This is pretty surprising for you, isn't it? I'm sorry."

"No no no no don't be sorry for being...you. I mean, yeah, I'm surprised. You were always so boy crazy."

"I don't know. I think I might have suspected back then and was overcompensating."

"Huh, who'd have thunk it. Into girls this whole time." Charlotte forced out several hard laughs.

When she got back to her duplex that night, she sat on her loveseat and stared at the wall. "Into girls this whole time," she repeated over and over to herself. Would it have mattered? She had tried so hard to hide her feelings, not wanting to destroy their friendship. She pressed her palms into her eyes. No. It didn't matter. The past was the past, and she couldn't change it. And it would have been so hard for them back then if they had been something more than friends. It was hard enough now. And this was okay. Even if Alyssa moved back, she was still going to be more than an hour away. They could be friends, nothing more, and it would be alright.

Charlotte sat in the passenger seat next to Alyssa staring down at her coffee. She had had to get up early as it was, but she had been unable to fall asleep for hours. Caffeine was pretty much the only thing keeping her from falling asleep through the service. The eulogies had been nice, of course, because one doesn't speak ill of the dead. They were on their way from the church to put him in the ground.

"Did you see Derrick in there?" Alyssa asked as the car crept down the one major thoroughfare through town.

"Yeah, he cleaned himself up pretty nice last year," Charlotte answered absently.

"Does he still hit on you mercilessly?"

Charlotte chuffed.

"Yeah, that didn't stop. Even after I came out as a lesbian. He keeps saying that I just haven't found the 'right guy yet.' As though he would be the one if that were the case." There was silence for a moment.

"Wait, what?" Alyssa, cast quick glances at her in confusion while still trying to keep her eyes on the road.

Charlotte tensed up. That's right. She had never actually talked about it. They had slipped back into everything so effortlessly she had taken for granted that Alyssa just knew.

"I uh, figured your mom would have mentioned it. I'm kinda, uh, gay." Silence again.

"How long?" Alyssa asked quietly.

"Fairly certain I was born that way...."

"You know what I mean..."

"I realized it probably...junior year? But I didn't actually try dating until after high school. I waited until I had finished my

Associate's degree and moved out before coming out to Mom and Dad. I'm out to everyone now." A beat of silence.

"How did everyone take it?"

Charlotte shrugged.

"I think Mom had figured it already because she was just kinda like 'okay.' Dad really freaked out, though. Kinda the reason I waited until I wasn't under his roof."

"And everyone else?"

"Well, I kinda came out slowly, so everyone kinda eased into it. I think it's possible that Dr. Kincaide fired me because of it, but I can't prove anything. Mostly people have been chill. Maybe weird occasionally. But it's not like I've ever actually brought a girl home or anything. I don't really date all that much. I have to go all the way into the city, and that makes things harder." Charlotte swung her head to look out the window. They were silent the whole rest of the way.

The coffin lowered, the prayers prayed, and the graces given, Alyssa was inundated with mourners before they could make it back to the car. She took each of them in turn giving them grim smiles of thank you for their well wishes. Alyssa's mom stood next to her, and mirrored her determination to not reveal how relieved they actually were that this was all over.

They got back into the car silently. Things were tense, and Charlotte knew it was her fault. She should have been more careful. This wasn't the time to have dropped such a bomb on Alyssa. Their friendship had weaknesses in it, after all, and it was starting to show.

They idled in front of the church where Charlotte had left her car after the service. She wanted to get out of the car and run off, but Alyssa was on the verge of wanting to say something. So, she waited.

"This is a weird time to ask about this, I know, but, if, uh, I, uh, move back to the city would you want to consider going out?" Alyssa said quietly. It took a moment for Charlotte to realize what she had proposed.

"Like...dating?"

"Yeah."

Charlotte stared ahead at a small crack in the windscreen. Her vision started blurring. Tears had formed along the rim of her eyes. No. This wasn't fair. Not after all this time. Not now.

"How dare you," Charlotte hissed. "How dare you do this to me? Is it really so easy for you? Did you think about how I might feel?"

Alyssa flashed confusion at her. She reached over to grab her wrist. Charlotte pulled it away. She blinked the tears out of her eyes and tumbled out of the car onto the

street. She didn't look back at her. She
couldn't do this.

There was a knock on her front door. It had
been two days. Alyssa was going back
tomorrow evening. Charlotte sat in the dark in
the living room, trying to focus on the late-
night television offerings. She had been in a
daze since the funeral, going to work, then
coming home, then sleeping. She just wanted
Alyssa to leave. She wanted everything to
settle back into what was normal.

"Charlotte." Alyssa's muffled voice from
the other side of the door. Charlotte didn't
answer. She closed her eyes and wished her
away. "I'm not leaving until you let me in. We
have to talk about what happened. I don't
want to leave without understanding. Please."
Charlotte waited another few moments. She
let out a deep breath, stood, and walked to the
door. She opened it, and Alyssa was standing
on the other side, arms across her chest, relief
dripping down from her head to her toes.
Charlotte turned and walked away across the
living room. She started to pace as Alyssa
came in and closed the door quietly behind
her.

"Did I do something wrong?" Alyssa asked
to Charlotte's back. "Should I not have

brought up the idea of dating? I just thought, well, I don't know what I thought. We both like girls, we're already friends, which is half of a relationship. Do you not think we'd be good together? Is it that you want to stay as friends? I just want to understand."

"You can't understand, Alyssa." Charlotte turned around hastily. "You just decided, one day, that you might like girls and went with it. What consequences did you suffer? Anything? You've never cared about what people think of you. That stuff slides off your back. It always has."

"What, so because you've been a lesbian longer, you think I haven't had to deal with stuff?"

"It's not about being gay."

"Then what's it about?" Alyssa had raised her voice and she squeezed her arms against herself tighter. "If don't want to date me, I get it, but I still don't understand why it's such a big fuss."

"I've wanted to date you since we were fifteen," Charlotte said sharply. Alyssa took half a step back in surprise. "And I don't know if I can take it," Charlotte continued. "It's just too much. What if it all goes wrong? All that time I struggled with these feelings alone won't have meant anything if it's just going to fall apart now." Charlotte started pacing again, unable to keep still. Alyssa moved her body around to make Charlotte face her.

"What about my feelings? After seeing you again and knowing that we have the same preference and wondering if, maybe, we weren't meant to be together or something...I'm just supposed to ignore that? I'm supposed to pretend that I don't feel something for you that I can't totally explain?"

"It's so easy for you." Charlotte pushed past Alyssa to pace some more. "Everything just seems to obvious. You see something you want, and you go after it. But it's more complicated than that."

"It doesn't have to be," Alyssa insisted. "I'm me and you're you and we've always been great together. If we like each other--"

"You left," Charlotte yelled, cutting her off. There was a pounding in her chest that she knew was her heart but felt like a wrecking ball smashing at the inside of her ribcage. "You left, and I got over it. I moved on. And I worked so hard. And now you're just...here...and you just stirred everything up for me, and you think things will always be the same. But it's *not* the same. You're not the same."

Alyssa's shoulders dropped and she clenched her hands to her chest. Charlotte played through their memories together. Had they ever fussed or fought like this before? Ever? Neither was quite sure how to react.

"You went out and you had all these wonderful adventures," Charlotte steamed on. "You found yourself out there in that huge world. And I didn't. I stayed here. And I didn't get the chance to change. At my core, I'm still the same girl I've always been, the one who suffered through her love for you. I denied who I was for years so that I could keep you in my life, because to be without you was worse than being who I really was. And when you left, I was actually relieved. I figured you'd never come back, and I was okay with that. I mean, really, who'd come back here if they had a choice? And if you were gone, I could be free. My feelings for you would fade, and, maybe, it wouldn't hurt quite so bad. But no. You had to come back. You had to just walk back into my life like it was nothing. But it's not nothing. Not to me." Charlotte collapsed onto the loveseat and rested her elbows on her knees. She entwined her fingers in her hair in exasperation. She felt weary.

"Do you know how hard it was to come back?" Alyssa said quietly.

Charlotte looked up at her. Alyssa was standing there with her hands on her hips, chest out and chin up.

"You're right. I did change. I discovered
things about myself, that I wouldn't have
learned if I had stayed here. I got perspective
on my life that I couldn't have gotten
otherwise. It was exactly what I needed."
Alyssa swallowed hard, then her body relaxed.
She sat on the floor cross-legged. "So to be
back here, this place I hate where I have all
these awful memories... I mean, I hadn't even
visited my own mother until now. I wasn't sure
I could do it. But you were here. And that
made it...okay. Because I knew you were here
and you'd be the same person that you'd
always been. The fact that you probably hadn't
changed is what gave me the strength to come
back to this place. I didn't know that it would
become like this. I didn't know that I would
have these feelings seeing you again. I
just....god...I feel like I'm in high school
again." Alyssa collapsed backward on the floor
and lay there with her arms spread out. Alyssa
closed her eyes and sighed.

As she watched her lie there, Charlotte
couldn't help but see it, that girl that she used
to know. Impulsive, a slave to emotions that
she didn't understand. Reckless. Optimistic.
She found herself standing. Her body lowered
itself next to Alyssa. They were so close to
each other. The air between them vibrated
with a soft heat. Charlotte crept her hand

closer to Alyssa's and gently took it in hers. It was warm. So warm. And soft. Alyssa slid a little closer to her. Their shoulders overlapped. They turned their faces toward one another at the same time. Their noses were touching. Alyssa kissed Charlotte. Quick. Fleeting. The heat lingered.

They were teenagers again, searching, trying to find a place in their small little part of the world. Despite everything, though, the world seemed even smaller than it ever had before. It was smaller than their town, smaller than their school, smaller than even the tiny block on which they had weathered so many blistering summers together. The future was starting to open. The flood of possibilities was washing through in wave after wave of uncertainty. What did these feelings mean? Were they just swept up in the drama of their newly formed emotions? They needed to figure out what would become of them, whether they could walk the world together.

But those things would have to wait, because, in that moment, their world was no bigger than that room, and they were the only inhabitants.

Toppings

Morven Moeller

The hats made the job so much worse than it had to be. Unlike the other workers, I couldn't pin it onto my buzzcut, so I had to hope that it didn't fly off in a wayward draft.

"Can you refill the soft-serve machines?" Tatianna, who pinned her hat to her braids, pushed the cart, laden with foodstuffs, through the little half-door on the far side of the kiosk. "I'll refill the toppings containers."

I nodded and pushed off the counter where I'd been leaning. I grabbed two of the jugs of ice cream mix from the bottom tier of the cart and pushed them clumsily onto the counter. It was only 11am, and while Tatianna was a morning person, I was not. She would argue that 11am wasn't morning, and I would glare at her half asleep until at least 2pm.

Tatianna and I had been friends since high school when we were both on the forensics team. We used to read poetry at each other over lunch, looking for pieces to submit for competitions. We read *Perfect* to each other on my granddad's front porch. And now, we shared an apartment around the corner from the university campus.

And while it wasn't my dream job, when Tatianna asked me to apply to work at the mall's ice cream kiosk with her, I had jumped at the opportunity. She was acting manager now that Kirsten had finished undergrad, so it was pretty sweet.

It sucked about as much as any other customer service job, but it felt like a step up from my part-time job as a busser at the pancake place. I still worked as a bartender three nights a week, and she still did her work-study program at the university library, but we made it all work.

Most weeks, working at the ice cream kiosk was the only time we really got to see each other.

I unscrewed the top of the vanilla soft serve machine, pulled out the spiral paddle and other removable pieces and put them in a bucket in the sink. I turned on the hot water to fill the bucket while I opened the other machines and gathered their parts.

By the time I was done sanitizing the machines, I was awake. Something about the temperature difference between the hot water and the cool metal threw my senses into overload and turned my brain on full power.

"Oh my god. Look at this banana." Tatianna turned around, a misshapen banana in her gloved hand. She pointed to a little extra growth at the top of it. "Look at its little penis!" She giggled.

Laughing, I joked, "I'm not sure that managers are allowed to say that to their employees."

She pursed her lips, knowing we'd both said far worse to each other on shift, then turned to keep stocking the cold case at the front of the kiosk. She'd finished with the candies, the containers filled to the marks on the outside in wobbly sharpie lines. She placed the fruits into the case, making sure that they were organized according to the picture taped to the underside of the lid.

I replaced the sanitized parts into the machines, poured in the ice cream mixes, and screwed the tops back on. "Mattie has a shift over at the calendar store this morning, yeah? She gonna stop by to say hi?"

Tatianna took the empty milk crate that had held cartons of strawberries back to the cart. She shrugged, "I mean, I think so. She hasn't told me that she wouldn't."

Tossing the emptied jugs into the sink, I smirked at her. "You guys gonna make out in the storage room again?"

"I hope not!" She shook her head, "I was freezing my titties off last time."

"I can imagine. It's cold storage. Doesn't Mattie find it cold?" I pushed the cart backward out the same half door it came in through.

Tatianna pulled the vinyl gloves off and dropped them into the trash can. "No." She shook her head disapprovingly, "but she's also the kind of person to wear basketball shorts in the snow."

"Yeah," I agreed.

It was Thursday, so there weren't that many people milling around the mall, and the people who were, were broke college students. The college students kept a steady pace at the booth, about two every 15 minutes. Not often enough to be busy, but not so few to feel bored.

The kiosk was on the third floor at the edge of the food court on the way to the college bookstore. It was prime real estate for our customer-base, offering a quick treat between cheap food court options and extortion-priced textbooks.

Like clockwork, Mattie stopped around three o'clock and whisked Tatianna away. For Tatianna's sake, I hoped it wasn't to the kiosk's storage room, but who could say.

I pulled a folding stool from the gap between the register counter and the half wall of the kiosk's perimeter, dropped onto it, folded my elbow onto the counter, and settled my chin into my palm.

It felt like our customers left when Tatianna left, and maybe they did. Maybe our customers are a steady stream of people who have little puppy crushes on the ice cream girl with the big curves and big smile. I was easily overlooked in comparison. I was too skinny and too pale and too pointy. Before the odd night out, Tatianna would grimace at my outfit, "You look straight wearing that," and push me back into my room to pick something else for me to wear.

It didn't feel fair since Mattie could show up wearing the same thing, but garnered the opposite reaction. But Mattie was the kind of lesbian that could pull off joggers and polos as queer fashion, and I was the kind of queer guy that looked like a closet case in the same.

Feeling bored for the first time all day, I pulled my phone out to tap around on Instagram. It was sure to sour my mood further, but it was the thing you did when you were bored.

Grumbling through my feed, I liked a few pics from some classmates who were at the beach and commented on one of my old English teachers' posts about the high school's homecoming dance preparations. I shared one of Tatianna's posts about an upcoming job fair at the library.

"Excuse me?"

Snapping up, I was met with the face of an exhausted but really cute person - guy according to a pin on his lanyard. He was wearing a black hoodie despite the heat, and his fingernails were painted dark, maroon red where they were steepled thoughtfully in front of his chest.

Dropping my phone to the counter, I shot up from where I had slumped over. "Hi! What can I get for you?" My smile was forced over my surprise, the same customer service smile that I'd used at any of my jobs.

"Yeah, uh," he looked up at the menu, scanning through it double-time. "What, uh, what would you recommend?" He drew his eyes back down, but avoided looking at me, skipping down to the toppings in the cold case.

Reaching into my usual customer service scripts, I waved a hand to the little easel sign on the counter. "Our most popular options are the small, two-topping cup and the two-topping shake, but as for the toppings, it's your choice. We have some fun combos listed on the glass if you need some inspiration." I pointed to the print-outs Tatianna had me cut out into hand-crampingly complex shapes.

The guy nodded and stepped further down the counter, looking at the options. I waited at the register, frozen, waiting for the next prompt.

He had a good profile, so I kept my eyes focused on that.

"I'll get the small cup with chocolate and whatever toppings you think are best." He shrugged off the decision, stepped back toward me, and reached for his wallet. It was attached to his pants by a chunky, silver chain in that peak 00s fashion.

I tapped the order into the register, completely on autopilot; it was the same order I rang up almost forty times a day. "Unfortunately, I can't pick your toppings for you. With allergies and intolerances, it's against our policy to pick." I pointed to the tap-to-pay device on the front of the register, and he obliged.

He tucked his card away. "Ah, makes sense."

Finishing out the order, I swiveled the screen around to him. He tapped at the tip options and signed on the screen.

I grabbed a cup and served up the usual two and a half swirls of ice cream, then turned to the toppings case. I stared at him; he stared at the case, fiddling with the buttons on the hanging end of his lanyard.

In a small voice, he asked, "So, hypothetically, what would you get on chocolate ice cream?"

Sinking into a hip, I shook my head. "I'm sorry, sir, but I can't pick your toppings."

He still didn't look at me, eyes trained down on the glass. "Oh." We waited in silence for a long moment. "Then, that'll be good."

"Huh?" I leaned forward to hear him better. He wasn't pointing to any of the toppings, his hands fiddling together in front of his chest. Training my eyes on what I could see of his face, I noticed that his ears were red, his nose was red. He was so red. Oh.

Whatever customer service fog had taken over my brain fell away. And I wasn't sure what to do, my usual scripts weren't prepared for this. "Uh. Okay." I held the ice cream out over the acrylic window.

He took it from me then glanced along the front of the kiosk. His shoulders hiked up further, and he mumbled something more.

I felt so bad, so out of my element, so embarrassed. I leaned even more forward. "I'm sorry, I couldn't hear that."

"Spoon," he said in a squeaky monotone.

"Oh!" I spun around, then spun back around again, because the spoons weren't behind me; they were in front of me, in a big box under the counter on the far side of the cold case. I pulled out a branded, color-change pink-to-blue spoon and held it out to him. "Here you go."

He swiped the spoon out of my hand and scurried off. I watched him go, kicking myself for being so dense, so dumb. This was why I was hopeless. He met up with a group of other students on the far side of the mezzanine, where most of them were looking in my direction. They continued on toward the bookstore, but not before giving me a round of dirty looks. One even flipped their middle finger at me.

I spent the rest of Tatianna's extended break thinking about it, replaying all the things I said and wishing that I wasn't such an asshole. Of course, I wasn't trying to be an asshole, but I was, and now I was in overdrive trying to figure out how to avoid being an asshole like that ever again.

We still had hours before close, but my brain was too busy to sit still, so I cleaned the kiosk. I wiped down the counters and the acrylic windows. I swept. I rinsed out the soft serve drip trays. I wiped down the register.

I wondered if it was too stalkerish to check for the guy's name from the receipt, decided that was indeed too stalkerish, then wondered if I was even more of an asshole for considering it.

"Woah. What's going on here?" Tatianna slid back into the kiosk. She didn't look like she'd just been humping her girlfriend in a storage closet, but she was good at hiding it. She looked at the near-sparkling kiosk. "Seriously, what's got you all riled up?"

As if all the anxious over-analysis had been a rehearsal for her return, the story fell out of my mouth, tripping over itself along the way. I scrubbed at some sticky-dried ice cream drips by the sink at the back corner of the kiosk. I felt better after telling Tatianna, but she hadn't said anything back to me yet, so my anxiety had shifted to focus on that.

"His name was Jaxson." There was a grin in her voice.

"What?!" I turned an unbelieving face to her.

She stood at the register, looking at the recent orders. She pointed to the digital receipt. "He tipped really good, too."

That information just made me feel worse. "No, did he really?" I felt like I was melting under the pressure of the situation. That made it all so much worse. "I'm a horrible person."

"No." She tutted. "Did you just get your girlfriend fired because you were caught half naked together in the Forever 21 backstock room? No, so you aren't a horrible person."

My worries were temporarily benched. "You guys were caught in the backstock room?"

Tatianna wasn't some troublemaker and never had been. She was a straight-A English major who worked at the university library part-time, but she was absolutely obsessed with her girlfriend. "Yeah." She drew it out, scrunching her face up in a sheepish expression. "She said that the only other people in the store were her two work-friends, but I guess one had called out sick and the manager was there to fill-in and happened to come back there."

Woah. Okay, maybe her day was a bit worse than my day. "What about Mattie?"

She deflated onto the stool. "She's upset that she lost her job, but she's mad at the manager, not me. But like," she put a hand to her forehead and closed her eyes in defeat, "if I were that manager, I would've fired her too."

I nodded, but didn't say anything. I wasn't sure there was anything I could say that would make that part of it better. I walked across the kiosk to throw the cleaning wipes I'd used into the trash and leaned against the counter over there. I stared at the floor, then, "So, where's Mattie? I'm surprised she didn't come back to harass us here."

Tatianna pinched at the bridge of her nose. "She was still yelling at the manager when I left." She let out a long sigh. "Why does dating have to be so difficult?" She said it mostly to herself, but I still felt it hit the pit in my gut.

"I wouldn't know." I huffed and crossed my arms. "I obviously flubbed up my chance with, what was his name?"

"Jaxson."

"I obviously flubbed up with Jaxson."

"No." Tatianna stood up and stomped over to me. "I might have had a bad day, but that doesn't mean that you have to have a bad day too." She checked her phone for the time. "I was gone for about an hour for my fifteen-minute break."

I stood up from my leaning. "That's not how-"

She shushed me by putting a finger over my mouth. "So, you've got plenty of time to go apologize." She'd brightened at her own idea. "You said they went over to the bookstore. Now, you can go over to the bookstore too. Find him, apologize, and sweep him off his feet." She clapped her hands onto my upper arms. "Yeah?"

I glared at her with a look that hopefully said 'that's a stupid idea' along the line of my eyebrows. "No."

"Why not?" She let go of my arms and dropped her shoulders in disappointment.

"Because no. That's a bad idea. He'd be there with all his friends, and what do I even say?" I crossed my arms tight over my chest, considering all the ways that it could go wrong.

Tatianna rolled her eyes. "I think you say sorry, then see where it goes from there." She tapped at the register, pulling up the employee roster for the day.

"Wait, I don't think I'm ready for that." I rushed across to block her from the register's screen, but she was stronger than I was, holding me back with a single arm.

She used her manager-override code to clock me out for my break. "I'll clock you back in after the 15 minutes is up, but don't feel like you have to be back." She pointed to the time in the top corner of the screen. "It'll probably pick up around dinner time, so try to be back by 6. Now," using the same strength she had before, she pushed me out of the kiosk's door, "get going before you think too much about it."

I stood there frozen just outside of the kiosk door.

"Get going." She pushed at my back again, serving to jumpstart my feet into walking toward the bookstore. "And don't get caught in the breakroom, turns out that doesn't go so well!" She called after me.

It was easy to find the group that Jaxson had been with. They were sitting in the cafe area with their laptops and textbooks strewn across three tables pushed together. They weren't working on the same stuff; I recognized a personal finance book and a collection of Shakespeare's plays in the mix. What I didn't see was Jaxson.

Losing all of my nerve, I took a hard right into the bookshelves across from the cafe. Who was I to think that they would be receptive to an apology, we weren't toddlers playing on the playground at recess. I squatted down and put my face in my hands. I felt exactly like a toddler right now.

"Hey, Ice cream boy!"

Was that me? That was probably me. I
froze and looked through my fingers at the
colorful book spines on the lowest shelf. I
wasn't focusing on them well enough to read
the titles, looking intensely at the space
between.

"Pink shirt, red hair, ice cream boy!"

That was very probably me.

"Get over here!"

Okay. I unfolded myself up and staggered
to the end of the bookshelf. I looked over
toward the cafe where one of the girls from
the group had come over to the railing
separating it from the bookstore area. She was
kneeling on one of the chairs and leaning on
the railing.

I pointed to myself stupidly.

She nodded condescendingly, like I was
the toddler I felt like, then made another
pointed look that said, 'Well, come on now.'

My arms wilted to my sides, and I walked
over to her. Since I was tall and she was
kneeling, I had to look down to look at her.

Her blue-lipsticked lips were screwed up,
obviously judging me. "So, what did you come
here for?"

Biting my lip, I briefly considered lying, but
that didn't seem like the right thing to do
under her righteous glare. "I was coming to

apologize?" It hadn't meant to be a question, but it certainly came out that way.

She sat back on her heels, making her even shorter. Her eyes flicked up and down over me. "Really?"

I nodded.

"Why? What do you think apologizing would do?" She didn't look as mad, but she was still curt, closed off.

Shrugging, I opened my mouth but didn't have an answer yet. My eyes roamed around the cafe area behind her, the air over each of her shoulders, her bright blue and purple hair. "I was in customer-service mode, and I didn't realize until it was too late." I cleared my throat. The other friends in the group in the distance had stopped typing, all glancing in our direction. Oh wow, this was so scary. "I feel like I was an asshole." I rushed to amend that, "I *was* an asshole."

She closed her eyes and nodded along, agreeing that I was an asshole.

"And, I mean, I was thinking that he was cute in my head, but I was just stuck in customer-service mode, you know?" I hoped that made sense.

Opening her eyes again, she didn't seem so cold. She waited a beat before sagging down from her protective posture. "Jax has thought you were cool for a while now. We kept nagging him to just go say hi to you or whatever, but he was so worried you weren't gay."

I felt very out of my depth.

She continued, "But like, you're dressed like that." She swept her eyes down again.

Following her gaze, I looked down at myself. I had forgotten about the dumb hat, so when it fell, I had to reach out to catch it. "This is my work uniform though." I looked back up.

Her eyes were on the hat in my hands, then flicked up to my confused gaze with a raised eyebrow. "A straight man wouldn't even try to wear that hat."

I looked down to the pink and white striped hat, wondering if that statement was universally true. I thought to the other employees at the ice cream kiosk, but the ones I knew were queer or femme, just kinda the tone of the place. Or maybe it was the pink and white striped hats? Without a counterargument, I nodded at the hat in my hands. "Actually, I'm bi."

"Huh," she replied noncommittally.

Dragging my gaze back up to the group, I looked at each of them. The guy with the Shakespeare book spoke up first, "Jaxson packed up for the day. He had to get to work."

"Oh." My eyes fell to the book instead of
the friend. "That's okay." The tone was far
from okay, but at least I'd relayed my
sentiment. Maybe he'd come by again another
day. "I should probably be getting back to the
kiosk soon anyway." I started to turn away.
"Could you tell him that I'm sorry?"

The girl looked disappointed, but it wasn't
directed at me, so that was a relief. "Yeah.
We'll tell him." The person with the finance
book paused where they were texting to offer
me a thumbs up, that was the same hand that
had flipped me off earlier.

Nodding once, I offered the group a sad
smile, then headed back out of the bookstore.

Tatianna didn't expect me back for a while,
and I didn't feel like going back yet, so I went
down the far escalators to walk around the
first floor of the mall.

I wasn't exactly sure how I felt. I felt better
since I'd kinda apologized, but I also felt
hollow since I hadn't gotten to apologize
directly. It was a wired, half-full kind of feeling
that had me shuffling around the first floor
with my hands dug deep into my pockets.

There was a group of young girls heading
into an accessory shop, though it still felt too
early for kids to be in the mall yet, but hey it

wasn't my business. There was a man in a business suit and shiny shoes, talking on his cellphone and walking at full speed toward the elevator. There was a slightly smarter man in an equally nice business suit paired with high quality sneakers, keeping pace behind him, probably carrying his fancy shoes in his shoulder bag.

When I turned the corner to the next wing of the mall, I spotted Mattie across the hall. I didn't wave at her or anything, not sure what kind of mood she would be in. She was propped up against a column with one of her legs bent so the sole of her foot was flat against the column too. She was looking at her phone, typing something rapidly. I abstractly wondered if she was stirring up shit.

Mattie wasn't a bad person. I really didn't think Tatianna would like her if she was, but Mattie was definitely a troublemaker. Usually, it was good trouble, like cussing out professors that deadnamed their students or petitioning the university to add black history as a 100-level option. She lifted her phone and pointed it toward the QR code on H&M's Now Hiring sign, then she settled back into the column, typing again. I felt like the people at H&M probably talked to the people at Forever 21, but maybe not. For Mattie's finance's sake, I was hoping not.

By the time I got to the department store
at the end of the floor, I was feeling a bit
better. I turned around and headed back the
way I came. I followed behind an older woman
who was trying, and failing, to hide the fact
that she had a dog in her bag. She kept
hushing the bag each time it barked, then she
would cough in a feeble attempt to cover up
the noise. From the look of the snout that kept
poking out the back of the bag, it looked like a
Pomeranian.

By the time I made it back to the center, it
was coming up on dinner time, so I really
needed to make my way back to Tatianna. I
looked up the stacked escalators, knowing that
the ice cream kiosk was almost directly in
front of where the top-most escalator let off.

I shrugged to myself, turned around, and
got in the line for Starbucks. The line moved
slowly, so I kept watching people. There were
some tables in the middle of the floor that
weren't specifically for Starbucks, but it was
mostly their customers using them.

Another man in a business suit, who had
propped his phone up on his Starbucks cup in
front of him, watched something while eating
a breakfast sandwich. The line moved forward.
A guy had fallen asleep in one of the massage
chairs with an accumulation of shopping bags
in his arms. The line moved forward. A little

kid closed their eyes and threw a coin into the fountain, then a moment later, plunged their hands in after it. The line moved forward.

I usually got the same thing, but I looked over the menu anyway. Sometimes I'd stray away to try one of their limited-edition drinks, but it never lasted long.

"Hi! Can I help who's next?"

I stepped around the family ordering at the first register. The girl behind the counter smiled at me, then her smile grew even bigger. I looked away since it looked creepy.

"Hi," she said again, "how can I help you?" Her voice was louder than before.

Swallowing, I pulled my wallet from my back pocket. "Yes, can I get a chocolatey-chip frappuccino?"

She keyed the order into the register. Their register seemed so much cooler than ours with its real buttons that made clicking noises when you typed. She pointed to the card reader, and I tapped my card.

I slid my card back into my wallet, then looked back up to her.

"Thanks," she said in the same loud voice as earlier. She turned away from me. "Hi! Can I help who's next?"

That felt abrupt. They usually asked me if I wanted the works, if I wanted whipped cream, if I wanted the java chips, if I wanted chocolate sauce. I mean, I always got it the same way, but I didn't think they knew me well enough to know my order.

The next customer had already stepped up, so I figured that I was going to get what I was going to get at this point. I stepped down to the waiting area, replaying the exchange. The barista called out someone's name, and I realized that she hadn't even gotten my name. How was this about to work? Did she ask and I answered automatically? I couldn't remember; I didn't think so.

I was working myself up, but with each name called out, I felt more like something had gone horribly wrong.

I was staring at my shoes when I heard a soft, "Hey, uh-"

That had to be mine. I stepped up to the counter in a rush to avoid receiving any annoyed looks from the other patrons, then looked up. It was Jaxson. Of course, it had to be Jaxson.

The tips of his ears were red, and he was looking fiercely at the cup. "Uh, what's your name?"

Suddenly, the shock was replaced by heat. I was sure that my ears were well on the way to matching my hair. "I'm Stanley." I had never regretted my name more; it felt so utterly clunky and uncool when it came out of my mouth. Out of all the names I could have picked, I had to choose my grandfather's.

Jaxson nodded, still not looking at me. He wrote my name on the side of the cup. "And, what toppings would you like?" He peeked up at me.

In the fastest and smoothest thinking I had ever done, I offered an apologetic smile, "Whatever you think is best." My voice trailed off at the end, suddenly thinking that it was probably super uncool to reuse the line that had caused so much turmoil earlier.

Offering a small grin in return, Jaxson nodded, "Alright. Let me get that ready for you." His red face ducked back behind the coffee machines, and I stepped back to get out of the other customers' way. Slowly, the bustling sounds of the Starbucks filtered back in, though I didn't know when they had filtered out.

After a few more drinks were called out and picked up, Jaxson stepped back out with my cup. "Stanley!" He looked right at me when he called it out, and then I liked my name again.

Shuffling forward, now feeling bashful, I took it from his hand instead of from the counter.

He flicked his eyes pointedly to the drink.

I looked at the drink. I didn't see anything out of the ordinary; it had all the usual toppings. "Looks good to me."

"Oh yeah," his voice cracked, "I'm great at topping." Then his eyebrows shot up. "Coffee. I'm great at topping coffee." He somehow got even redder. "Coffee toppings."

My eyes were tearing up at how hot my face was, and I really couldn't say anything back, so I nodded furiously and ran away, cutting in front of a dad trying to fold a stroller, to run up the escalator.

Oh No! It's a Lacy Thong!!!

Zahra Jons

Wyatt offered a tight smile to the other two men sitting at the breakfast table. There was Tucker, the best man, and Kade, the groom's younger cousin. The groom, Stephan, was at the stove, flipping pancakes. A platter of bacon and a dish of caramelized apple slices were already on the table.

He had to admit, the food smelled heavenly.

The wedding was next Saturday, and this men's breakfast was the lead up to this Saturday's stag party.

"C'mon, man. Hurry up!" Tucker rocked back on his chair. "We're wasting daylight."

"What's your hurry?" Stephan expertly flipped the last pancake in the pan, not even needing to watch to make sure it landed nice and flat and on the proper side.

"We've got things to do. Sexy stuff to buy."
Tucker waggled his eyebrows.

Wyatt stifled his groan. *What did they have
to buy that would be sexy?*

Stephan set the platter of pancakes on the
table. "We have to buy what?"

Tucker snorted. "You need to buy your
bride a wedding-night gift." He grabbed the
serving fork and plopped three pancakes on
his plate, dousing them with the sticky, saucy
apple topping.

Kade sighed and reached for the fork for
the pancakes. He looked like Wyatt felt.

Maybe Wyatt could bluff his way out after
breakfast.

"So, Kade," Tucker spoke around a mouth
stuffed with apples and pancake, "you still
swim?"

Kade froze mid-apple-syrup drizzle and
glanced at Wyatt, eyes growing wide. "Uh, no,
not since I graduated high school."

"Shame. You were real good." Tucker
crumbled a couple slices of bacon over his
pancakes. "Didn't your team win all-city one
summer?"

"Um, yeah." Kade's voice came out a bit
high-pitched and he cleared his throat, the
timber of his voice dropping. "We got second
place a couple summers, too."

"Oh?" Wyatt grinned. Swimming was something he could talk about, something he could talk about a lot. He'd spent summers on a swim team, himself. Coming in second only to the Krakens. "I swam on a team here locally. I was a Marlin for six summers, starting in middle school."

Kade's face seemed to pale and his eyes got even wider.

"Hey," Tucker munched on a strip of bacon, "what was your team's name, Kade? The Octopuses? The Squids? Something like that?"

"Kraken." Kade's voice cracked. "I was a Kraken."

Stephan stood up, thighs bumping against the table. "Hey, are we finished? We need to get going if Tucker is going to lead us on this foray to the mall."

Wyatt didn't have a chance to bail on the plan; before he could catch a breath to voice an excuse, he was crammed into the back seat of Tucker's orange 2020 Challenger, right knee brushing Kade's left, head bumping against the headliner.

Happily, it was a short drive to the mall.

Unhappily, Tucker made it even quicker.

Kade was thrown into Wyatt's side three times; Wyatt thrown toward him, four.

"Jeez, Tucker," Wyatt braced himself against the front headrest, "the mall's not going anywhere."

Heaving a deep sigh once they'd found a decent parking space in the north parking garage, Wyatt was happy to climb out of the cramped back seat. "I think I might have had more room in Stephan's truck."

"Yeah," Tucker grinned and winked, "I know."

Wyatt sighed and followed the three men into the mall, dragging his feet. He hated shopping.

The mall was not too busy since it was only just going on eleven, although small pods of teens were roaming around, heading for the escalators and the theater on the top floor.

The ground floor was almost empty, save for a group of older women power walking in a two-across formation.

Wyatt cast a longing glance toward the gaming store that was still not open. The COMING SOON sign was yellowing on the frayed edges and he could see products on about half the shelves.

Kade caught his gaze and made a sympathetic face. They both sighed and caught up with the other two.

Yup. Victoria's Secret was the last place Wyatt thought he'd be spending a Saturday. It

was full of pink and lace and fluff
and...and...*women.*

Tucker bound into the store, leading the
charge, his laughter ricocheting off the walls,
dragging Stephan behind him. It seemed the
best man would thoroughly enjoy their visit to
lady-land.

Kade stood back, eyeing the mannequins in
the window display like they bore weapons.

There was something about that look...

Wyatt knew from the breakfast
conversation that at some point, for at least
one summer if not several, he and Kade had
swum against each other. But for the life of
him, he could not remember seeing Kade at
any swim meet. The Krakens and the
Marlins—to this day—were keen rivals for the
all-city summer swim trophies, trading first
and second places every other season or so.

And they were the same age, or pretty
darn close; Stephan had mentioned that Kade
was a Junior at Virginia Tech. Wyatt was a
Junior at William and Mary.

Which meant, he really should remember
Kade. The young man was handsome, his
jawline well-defined but not overly sharp, his
nose long and straight, his dirty-blond hair
curling over his ears and at the nape of his
neck. His eyes were that perfect hazel that
seemed to change color with the clothes you

wore; the blue sweatshirt he'd pulled on over his t-shirt had turned what had been green eyes at breakfast into soft gray orbs now.

There was no way he could have forgotten Kade. He'd realized in ninth grade that he was attracted to guys—and Kade was the kind of guy he would have been attracted to, even back then.

Honestly, Tucker was attractive, too. He'd even had a crush on him in his sophomore year of high school. Tucker, Stephan, and Renee—the bride-to-be and Wyatt's sister— had all hung out together, listening to music and watching movies every Friday night in the basement den.

Of course, Renee had figured it out as soon as it manifested and teased him mercilessly for a whole year, which may have helped him get over his crush. She'd only really stopped the teasing when she'd graduated high school—as valedictorian no less—and gone off to university in Boston.

His sister was only a couple years older than he was, and they'd been close growing up. He'd never had to tell her he liked boys, as well as girls—which had eventually morphed into pretty much only liking boys—and she'd never been mean with her teasing. Heck, he'd teased her back just as much—especially about Stephan.

Wyatt had been almost as happy as his sister when she announced her engagement to Stephan; those two were great together. Everyone had been certain it would happen. Uncle Charles (their dad's brother) had even tried to set up a betting pool about it until his sister (their mom) found out and stopped it.

Stephan was family. Hell, Tucker was family.

Which was why he'd agreed to be a groomsman at the wedding.

There wasn't much he wouldn't do for his sister. Or Stephan.

But standing around a Victoria's Secret while Tucker tossed lacy bits of unmentionables at Stephan while talking about said sister might be where he had to draw the line.

The young woman behind the counter slid her gaze down the forms of Stephan and Tucker, and then those of Wyatt and Kade, and smiled, straightened her shirt and fixed her hair. Her upbeat greeting to their group was met by a flirtatious smile from Tucker and an eye roll from Kade.

Wyatt understood the woman's reaction. While he was over his crush on Tucker, the man did draw wanton looks from women and men alike. Kade, it seemed, did as well.

Oh, yes. Tucker and Kade were both handsome—Wyatt would never deny that. Getting to watch them was almost enough to make the glittery pink-lace environment worthwhile.

And while Tucker was loud and obnoxious and always poking fun at everything and everyone, Kade seemed quiet, offering that soft smile to Wyatt. And he seemed to think before speaking, unlike Tucker, who hadn't stopped talking since before they'd even gotten their coffee. Kade had said maybe a dozen words since they'd all put their spent coffee cups and syrup-laden plates in the dishwasher.

And now...

"Hey, check this one out!"

Wyatt leaned his head back and stared cross-eyed at the scrap of lace Tucker shoved into his face.

"Your sister would look hot in this." The man waggled his eyebrows at Wyatt.

"Tucker," Stephan poked at his best man's shoulder, "leave him alone. Pretty sure he doesn't want to think about his sister in a thong."

"Fine." Tucker spun around and waved the bit of fabric around at the other groomsman. "Any girl would look good in this, right?" He elbowed Kade and snickered, winking and wiggling his hips. "Right?"

Taking a step away from his companions, Wyatt tried to offer a thankful smile to Stephan, and one of commiseration with the man's cousin, but it missed both marks when Tucker barked a laugh and they both winced and closed their eyes.

Wyatt couldn't quite understand how he came to be here, a full week before his sister's wedding. He was a groomsman, sure, but this was a little more than he'd signed up for. The stag party, and all that it entailed, was going to be that night, at Tucker's apartment, and if the day kept going as it was, Wyatt was not going to be feeling up for any sort of party later.

It looked like the other groomsman shared his opinion on the outing. Kade was staring wide-eyed at a busty mannequin adorned in a glittery corset, cheeks becoming a darker pink.

When Tucker pointed at a barely-there push-up corset and whispered something to Stephan that had the man flushing like a beet, it only got worse. Wyatt just couldn't understand why the best man was so enthralled with the bras, panties, and other unmentionables on display. Couldn't he see that he was embarrassing all three of them?

Did women get this weird when they looked at the boxers on the mannequins at H&M? Wait—where exactly did one go to buy sexy, lacy unmentionables for the groom? Was there such a thing as lacy briefs for men?

Maybe he'd have to ask Renee. Later...much, much later. Like sometime after her tenth wedding anniversary.

Wandering away from the two boisterous men, Wyatt tried to look at the softer stuff—a pair of fluffy sloth slippers and a soft pink robe with "lover-girl" in script on one lapel. He had no issues imagining his sister in these.

"Does Renee like slippers?" Stephan asked, right at Wyatt's shoulder, making him jump and squeak. *Please don't let Tucker—or Kade—have heard that.*

"I mean...she wears them." Wyatt shrugged and swallowed and shifted away from the older man.

Tucker snorted. "Steph, why you wanna buy her sloths?" His chortle drew the gaze of cashier and Wyatt wanted to sink into the floor at the scathing glare she leveled in their direction.

Steph sighed and picked up a pair of slippers, fingers stroking over the fuzzy face. "Why not? If she likes them. Kade, what do you think?"

Snorting, Tucker shook his head. "Don't go asking him." The best man grabbed the slippers out of his hands and tossed them back onto the shelf. "Sloths are not sexy, dude."

Wyatt really didn't want to be part of this conversation; younger brothers should not be subjected to arguments over what made their older sister sexy. He sidled farther away, eyeing the exit. There was a pretzel place just down the mall; maybe he could sneak out and-

"Wyatt? Wyatt Baker?" A high-pitched feminine voice called out from somewhere.

Oh, shit. That was Amanda Graham's voice.

Groaning, Wyatt turned to look in the direction the voice had come from. "Hi, Mandy." He offered a little wave that said *I'm acknowledging your presence but really hoping you'll go away.*

She didn't get the message.

Amanda was the executive assistant's assistant at Baker, Baker, and Michaelson, the law firm his dad had started with his two uncles more years ago than Wyatt could count. He'd interned there the summer right after high school, when he'd still been considering following in his father's legal footsteps.

The slightly older young woman—she'd been in the grade between him and Renee at high school—had been very vocal about how cute she thought Wyatt was and how much she wouldn't mind going on a date. There had been a lot of eye-lash batting and soft purring in his presence.

He hadn't been anywhere near as enamored with her, which had made him think he really wasn't bi, and had told her he was gay. He had hoped it would make her back off without involving HR.

And it did.

But she'd also promptly told his dad's executive assistant and legal secretary and his paralegal and...

He'd been still figuring himself out and hadn't told anyone else. Been still in the closet, so to speak. The only person besides himself that had had any inkling that he wasn't anything but straight had been Renee—and she hadn't let on to anyone else.

But then, he'd had to tell his dad and his mom. They'd only smiled and explained that they'd figured it out some time ago and that all they cared about was that he was happy and safe.

And his dad had hung a gay pride flag in his office.

Now, the young woman sauntered in, trailing her fingers over the display of silky panties in a bin near the front of the store. "This is the last place I'd ever think to find you." She cocked her head to one side, glaring at him through slitted eyes.

"Oh?" He almost managed to control the stammer. "I'm here as a member of my sister's wedding party."

Please, please, please, go away.

But she only stalked closer. "Bridal party?"

"I'm a groomsman. In Renee's wedding. Representing our family for the guys." He shrugged and frowned at her. "You know my sister, Renee, right? She's Mr. Michaelson's legal secretary."

Renee was the only one of his parents' four children that had gone into the legal profession, and she wasn't even a lawyer.

"Okay, yeah, I know your sister." She leaned in close. "But why are you here?"

"Um, well," Wyatt shuffled back, bumping the mannequin behind him, "her fiancé is looking for a gift. You know, for the wedding night."

She smirked. "And what do you know about wedding nights?"

Wyatt frowned. "Nothing, I suppose. But since I'm a groomsman..." He shrugged. He couldn't really answer a question he didn't know the answer to.

Kade stepped up. "We're here for moral support." He jabbed a thumb over his shoulder at Stephan and Tucker. "And I suspect to try to help Stephan pen Tucker in when he gets too much."

Mandy looked over Kade's shoulder, craning her neck to see. "Too much of what?"

"Too much of Tucker." Chuckling, Kade glanced back at his cousin, who was now furiously trying to grab a hot pink garter from his friend's hand.

Mandy glanced over at the two other men in their group and sucked in a soft gasp. "Is that Tucker Browne?"

Kade smirked and shook his head at the two men. "The one and only—I hope."

Wyatt smothered his snicker.

But Mandy was eyeing her new target, and in a way that made Wyatt's stomach queasy. He caught Kade's gaze and jerked his head toward the store exit.

Kade nodded and the pair slid around Mandy and a couple of young women they hadn't been introduced to and escaped to the common concourse between the shops.

Once outside, Wyatt tugged his phone out of his back pocket and texted Stephan that he and Kade were going to grab a snack. And to beware because Mandy was in the store and on the prowl. Stephan knew Mandy; he was in his final year of studying law and had interned several times at the firm.

"So...Starbuck's?" Kade pointed down the mall to the deep green and white kiosk in the center with only a short line of folx waiting.

"Sure." Wyatt pulled up the app on his phone. "I think I have points we can use."

"Oh, um...you don't have to—" Kade's cheeks tinged a deeper pink. It was still cute.

Wyatt grinned and shrugged. "Hey, I usually forget to use them and they run out. You're kinda doing me a favor by letting me treat."

Kade only raised a brow at him, but led the way through the crowd to the end of the not-too-long line. They'd just placed their orders and paid—a maple chai latte for Kade and a mocha cappuccino for Wyatt—when a familiar voice called out a greeting.

"Hey, Wyatt!" Jaxon Cleary worked at the Starbuck's and, though he was no longer wearing the apron, it was draped over the back of his chair. He sat at a table across from somebody Wyatt felt he ought to recognize but didn't from behind; hey—he wasn't really a back-of-the-neck man.

Jaxon grinned and waved them over.

That somebody spun around and grinned. "Wy-att!? Jeez, I haven't seen you since the summer after graduation!"

"Hey, Stanley. Good to see you." Wyatt clapped a hand on Stanley's shoulder and grinned. "Still working at the ice cream place upstairs?"

Stanley stood and hugged Wyatt, pulling him up to his tiptoes and making him laugh. "Yup. Where else would I work?" They let go of Wyatt and tapped a fist lightly on his arm. "Beard looks good on you."

Wyatt flushed. "Yeah, thanks." He rubbed his jaw, feeling the short hairs that grew there. "Didn't think I'd ever be able to grow anything worthwhile."

He gestured to Kade to introduce him but—

"Chai latte for Kate! Kale?? Something with a K. Mocha capp for Wytt—er—W-y-a-tt?"

Kade gasped and froze. The young man tensed and spun to look at whoever had just shouted. His face had paled, his mouth dropping open in a stunned 'o'.

"Fucking..." Stanley breathed out the word, the syllables harsh in their throat. "Why can't folks learn to spell?"

"Hey, ease up guys, mistakes happen. I'll go get our drinks, yeah?" Wyatt clapped a light hand on Kade's shoulder, grinning, and ambled over to the pick-up counter, smiling at the harried crew still making coffees and taking more orders. He glanced down at the cups, looking for his mocha and the chai for—

wait—Kate...Kate Miller. Kate Miller, star swimmer of the Krakens.

Kate Miller who'd been on the mixed relay team every year the Krakens had one that particular race against the Marlins.

Shit. Fuck.

Kade...Miller.

Who was a swimmer. Tucker had said as much that morning.

Maybe it was a brother...or a cousin?

But...no. It wasn't. He could see it now. And by Stanley's reaction to the mistakenly called name...the deadnaming...he was right.

Wyatt sucked in a breath, swallowed, and stared at the drink cups, the black ink names smudged and sloppy on the label. He could see how easy it had been to read the names wrong. He picked them up, setting them back down to adjust the lid tighter on his mocha, then picked them back up to head over to his friends.

Kade had pulled a couple extra chairs closer and was sitting in one, hands folded on the table, talking to Stanley, but his eyes would flick over to Wyatt then dart back. Color had come back to his face and he wasn't as tense.

"Here you go. The label says chai latte so I'm pretty sure they just fucked up the name." Wyatt smiled.

"Yeah." Kade's voice rasped, accepting the hot spicy-sweet tea. "Surprising how often that happens."

"So," Stanley drummed their fingers on the table, "you two on a date or what?"

Kade flushed and closed his eyes.

Wyatt choked on his sip of caffeinated chocolate heaven. "No! We're here with Stephan and Tucker."

Jaxon looked around pointedly, chuckling wide-eyed. "You are?"

Kade, eyes now open and the pink receding, chuckled and shook his head. "We abandoned Stephan to Tucker back at Victoria's Secret." He snickered and set his chai down so as not to spill it. "Tucker was trying to convince him to buy his fiancé a red lace thong."

"Fiancé?" Stanley raised their brows. "Stephan's getting married?"

"Yeah." Wyatt took a careful sip, glad of the turn in conversation. Kade wasn't necessarily interested in guys and he didn't want them to feel any more uncomfortable. "To my sister, Renee. I thought everyone knew."

"No." Stanley shook his head. "Guess I'm a bit out of the loop." Then... "Congratulations, I guess."

Jaxon frowned. "But why are you two here?" From the slowly fading look of horror on his face, he understood the trauma Wyatt had gone through earlier.

"We're groomsmen. Tucker's the best man, of course." Wyatt shrugged. "I'm representing the Baker family."

"Stephan's my cousin." Kade took a sip of his drink and sighed. "Not sure why he chose me instead of one of my older brothers. I guess Tucker insisted."

Stanley raised a brow. "Tucker Browne insisted you be a groomsman?"

Kade shrugged.

"Probably because I'm one, and Kade and I are similar in age. And we're both into swimming." Wyatt swiped at his chin where his mocha was leaking out under the lip. "Summer league. Kade was a Kraken. And you both know I was a Marlin."

Stanley laughed. "There gonna be swimming at the wedding?"

Wyatt sighed and shot a dark look at his friend. "Well, no." He smirked. "But there is an Olympic-sized pool at the hotel where the reception will be held."

Kade pushed gently at Stanley's shoulder. "I think it's just that we have something in common, you know?" He spun his near-empty cup on the table. "We have something we can talk about during the boring bits."

Jaxon snickered. "Since when did Tucker Browne care about other folks having stuff to talk about?"

Wyatt raised a brow, as did Kade.

Stanley tapped the tabletop and snorted. "Jaxon's sister, Brie, dated Tucker for a while in her senior year."

"Ah." Wyatt nodded. "I remember." He'd been so jealous of the girl; he'd caught Tucker kissing her in the stairwell at school on several occasions.

"He's not that bad, you know." Kade glanced over at Wyatt and licked his lips. "He knows about...me." The young man shrugged. "Treats me the same he always has, maybe even more...guyish...now, you know. I mean, he's NEVER deadnamed me."

Wyatt smiled, his chest warming at the trust Kade just gave him. "Tucker does have a good side to him—when he wants to show it." No matter the soft story Kade had just shared, he was NOT going to share how gentle Tucker had been with him when his first college relationship had ended when the guy had revealed he'd only been dating Wyatt to gain access to his father's law firm. Hell, Tucker had even told him he'd think Wyatt was cute if he was gay and to just forget about the guy because he wasn't worth the energy it took to be mad at him.

Snickering, Stanley rose from their chair. "If you say so. I gotta go. My shift starts at one."

Jaxon stood up, too, stretching and picking up their apron from the back of their chair. "I'll walk you up, then head home. I only picked up a couple hours opening this morning."

The two waved, meandering toward the escalators, holding hands.

"I didn't know they were a couple." Wyatt smiled at them over his shoulder. He turned back to Kade. "They look good together."

Kade nodded. "They do."

"Dudes." Tucker dropped into the chair Jaxon had just vacated.

Stephan sat in the other empty chair, a large pink and black boutique bag in one hand. "That was most painful."

"C'mon." Tucker kicked at Stephan's leg under the table. "It wasn't that bad. And I let you buy those sloth slippers."

Snorting, Stephan rested his forehead in his hands, his elbows supporting from the table. "Only after I bought the damn thong...and the bath bombs and the...that other thing."

Tucker laughed but said no more. "You guys doing okay?" He glanced from Kade to Wyatt and back again.

"Yeah. We were talking to Jaxon and Stanley. Went to high school with them." Wyatt made to take a sip of his coffee but it was empty. He glanced to the line at Starbucks. It was a little longer than it was when they'd first arrived. "Anyone want a drink?"

Stephan shook his head while Tucker squinted at the menu.

"Kade?" Wyatt tilted his head at him.

"No, I'm good." He smiled.

Tucker stood and grabbed Wyatt's arm. "Let's go."

They waited at the end of the line, Tucker staring up at the menu with a wrinkled nose. "They have just regular old coffee, right?"

Wyatt's sigh was soft. "Yes. You can just ask for a cup of coffee."

Tucker nodded.

They remained quiet and shuffled ahead three steps.

"So," Tucker checked him in the shoulder, "what do you think of Kade?"

Huh? What?

"I mean, he's nice." Wyatt stared at Tucker.

Tucker swayed and shuffled forward, then leaned close to whisper. "He's single. Just so you know."

Oh, *fuck*. Is Tucker matchmaking?!?

"...and, I heard you're still single." Tucker side-eyed him. "At least, Renee hasn't heard about anyone."

Wyatt groaned. "No, there's isn't anyone." He prodded Tucker ahead into the newly created space in front of them. A couple more orders and they'd be at the register. "You know what you want?"

"Yeah. Coffee." Tucker retrieved his wallet and pulled out a twenty, holding it up. "I got this."

Kade and Stephan sat at the table, talking. Every so often, Kade's gaze drifted to Wyatt and his cheeks would tinge pink.

"Just so you know, I didn't hire a stripper for the party." Tucker frowned at the array of food on display, tapping the case over a chocolate chip cookie. "That looks good."

"Um, yeah." Wyatt glanced at the cookie. "It's got nuts in it, though."

"Oh." Tucker sniffed.

"No stripper?"

"Nope." Leaning forward, Tucker checked out the chocolate croissant. "Don't want you guys uncomfortable. I do have beer and cider, though, and wings and chips and stuff. And some blow up mattresses so you can crash at my place if you need to."

Wyatt pointed at the space in front of the register.

Tucker grinned at the barista. "I'll take one of those chocolate pastries and a coffee...grande? Wyatt, what do you want?"

"Grande mocha cappuccino. Hot."

After getting his change, the pair moved to the pick-up end of the counter.

Wyatt watched Kade some more, absently listening to Tucker read off the types of coffee beans on display for sale.

"What the fuck is dark roast hazelnut toffee whole bean coffee?" Tucker picked up a bag and frowned at the description.

"It's a specialty flavored coffee. Pretty good. But since it's whole bean, you need a grinder at home."

Tucker set the bag back and heaved a deep sigh. "Kade's a good kid."

Wyatt blinked. "He's not a kid."

"No, I suppose not." Tucker stepped forward to accept the bag that contained his pastry.

Their coffee was still in the works.

They waited, not speaking. Not exactly patiently. Tucker bounced one foot and crinkled the bag in his hand.

"I kinda hoped you two might hit it off."
Tucker's name—or a close facsimile of it—was
called and two cups were set on the counter.
"You and Kade. I know you swam against each
other when you were in high school."

Wyatt picked up their drinks, smiling at the
barista. "Thanks." He nodded toward the
table.

Tucker leaned close again. "Don't tell
Stephan."

"Huh?"

"About the no stripper thing. I haven't told
him and I'm trying to keep him wondering."
Tucker pulled the pastry from the bag and
took a bite, licking the chocolate off his lip.
"You know, can't have him thinking he's
getting off easy getting married and all."

"Ah, okay." Wyatt grinned. "What are we
going to do then?"

"Play an RPG. I found one online that's all
about a bunch of guys trying to get their friend
to the church for his wedding, but there's an
alien invasion and they have to fight their way
through a battle to get there."

Wyatt laughed. "Battle and beer?"

"Yup." Tucker took his coffee cup. "You
CAN tell Kade, though. Kinda want both of you
comfortable, you know. Don't want you to
duck out when you don't have to."

"Okay." Wyatt grinned.

They finished the short walk to the table and took their seats.

"Are we done buying sexy stuff?" Stephan rolled his head to glare at Tucker.

"Nah. We gotta get you something, too."

Stephan gasped and wheezed out, "What the fuck?"

Kade snorted then collapsed into giggles.

"Dude. I know all you own is tightie-whities. We need to find you something else." Tucker popped the last of the croissant in his mouth and chased it with half his coffee. "Add some," he waggled his brows, "let's say...color down there."

Kade hid his face in his hands, his giggles muffled. "Where are we supposed to find sexy men's underwear?"

Wyatt sipped at his drink and snickered. "H&M has colored briefs but...not sure I'd call them sexy."

Tucker tipped his chair back and finished his coffee. "Sexier than plain old-man knickers."

Stephan flushed and Wyatt shook his head. Earlier, he'd been pissed off at Tucker's antics, but now, knowing that this was it, that there wasn't going to be an embarrassing stripper moment for his soon-to-be brother-in-law later on, he wasn't. In fact, he was inclined to play along with Tucker.

Wyatt smirked. "I think I saw a mesh pair the last time I was in there."

Tucker nearly fell out of his chair.

Kade stared at Wyatt, a frown forming on their face.

"Well," Stephan stood, defeated, and picked up the bag he already had, "let's get this over with."

The H&M was on the second floor, within line of sight of the ice cream kiosk on the third floor. Stanley was staring at them, shaking their head while handing over a cup of rolled ice cream.

Wyatt waved and grinned.

Despite his statement of getting this over with, Stephan dragged his feet. "Are we sure we want to do this?"

Tucker tugged on his friend's elbow. "'course we do."

Kade was distracted by a selection of muted, leaf-patterned chinos on display near the front of the men's side of the store.

Wyatt leaned toward Kade's ear, watching Tucker drag Stephan toward the back. "Tucker said to let you know there isn't going to be a stripper at the party."

"What? There isn't?" Kade dropped the price tag he was reading.

"Nah. Said he didn't want us uncomfortable—and he knew it would embarrass Stephan. He's found what sounds like a fun RPG to play."

"An RPG?" Kade chuckled and watched the two men bicker next to a headless mannequin sporting form-fitting red briefs.

"Yeah. It's about a bunch of guys getting attacked by aliens on the way to a wedding."

Kade snickered. "Sounds appropriate anyway."

"Yup."

The other man looked at him directly, and Wyatt could see the brown and green and gray in his irises undulate. "I know why I'd be uncomfortable. Why would you be?"

"Oh, I'm..." Wyatt swallowed. Should he say he was gay? Was he gay? Yeah, he was attracted to masculinity, but... "I'm pan. Mostly been dating men...well," he cleared his throat, "masculine-leaning folks."

Blinking, Kade took in a breath loud enough that Wyatt could hear its rasp. It rushed back out, too "Masculine-leaning?"

Wyatt nodded. And waited.

Kade smiled, hard enough his eyes crinkled and a little dimple appeared in his cheek. "Cool."

CPSIA information can be obtained
at www.ICGtesting.com
Printed in the USA
LVHW042206270323
742731LV00030B/1213